CW00631318

the cat's whiskers

[New Zealand writers on cats]

the cat's whiskers

[New Zealand writers on cats]

and dispose of [illegible]
I have so little time
I am afraid I will not
get rid of many.
The Black Devil has
grown in to such a
beautiful Cat tho' in
spite of its beauty nobody
seems to care much about
[illegible]
this hardly does the
darling justice and
I have certainly
given it more
than its share of
whiskers.
[illegible]
Have you done many
sketching? [illegible]

Edited by Peter Wells

V

The cat's whiskers : New Zealand writers on cats
/ edited by Peter Wells.
Includes index.
ISBN 1-86941-745-3
1. Cats—Fiction. 2. Cats—Poetry. 3. Short stories, New Zealand.
4. New Zealand poetry—21st century. 5. New Zealand
essays—21st century. I. Wells, Peter, 1950-
NZ820.803629752—dc 22

A VINTAGE BOOK
published by
Random House New Zealand
18 Poland Road, Glenfield, Auckland, New Zealand
www.randomhouse.co.nz

First published 2005

ISBN 1 86941 745 3

Text design: Janet Hunt
Jacket design: Matthew Trbuhovic
Jacket illustration: Frances Hodgkins' letter to Isabel Hodgkins featuring the Black Devil, her cat [ca 7 May 1892], Alexander Turnbull Library, Wellington, New Zealand
Printed in China by Everbest Printing Co Ltd

contents

Cats I Have Known

Poems

Short Stories

Poems

Cats I Have Known

Poems

introduction

I can never speak of cats without a sentiment of regret for my poor Trim, the favourite of all our cat's company on the Spyall. This good natured purring animal was born on board His Majesty's ship the Roundabout in 1799 during a passage from the Cape of Good Hope to Botany Bay . . .

We do not have any New Zealand books, as far as I know, such as the entrancing tale that Captain Flinders wrote in 1809 about his cat, Trim. Written as a form of mock essay, 'A Biographical Tribute to the Memory of Trim' follows the history of the ship-borne cat as Flinders circumnavigated Australia. Finally, the unfortunate mog disappears, leaving behind a bereft captain.

The motif of a cat arriving by ship is one that appears equally relevant to New Zealand. George Llewellyn Meredith recorded in *Adventuring in Maoriland* (1872) what must have been an all-too-familiar tale of the adventures in the life of a ship's cat. A small terrier let loose aboard found the ship's cat, 'who turned round, spat at the pup, and boxed his ears, with her claws much in evidence. As the cat turned away in disgust, the pup caught hold of the end of her tail . . . Puss then jumped up on the taffrail, and the pup put his forepaws up against the bulwarks, apparently to play Romeo to her Juliet; whereupon the cat jumped into the sea. In about one minute poor pussy was quite one hundred yards astern, and a huge albatross swooped down on her. Goodbye, pussy.' A cruel fate indeed for such a newly introduced species.

When Joel Samuel Polack published a book in 1838 called *New Zealand: Being a Narrative of Travels and Adventures During a Residence in that Country Between 1831 and 1837*, he estimated that the cat had already been in New Zealand for quarter of a century, brought here by whalers. The tale of that first cat down the gangplank would be a fascinating one. Polack noted that the puhihi (Maori for pussy-cat) was alleged to be 'very nutritious', no doubt a summation of more than a few cats' fate in islands so starved of protein. Dieffenbach, in 1843, reported that local cats had already become wild — they had reverted to 'the streaky grey colour of the original animal when in a state of nature'. They were also decimating native birdlife and valuable introduced species, according to the gimlet-eyed German.

The wildcat soon came to represent many things particular to colonial life. Mark Twain, visiting us in 1897, talked amusingly of the absence of 'the moral fabric of the [local] cat'. At Bluff he had noted tomcats attacking rabbits, and he wrote 'the cat found with a rabbit in its possession does not have to explain — everybody looks the other way.' In *My New Zealand Garden by a Suffolk Lady* in 1902, the lady author referred to 'my affectionate tomcats [being] very fond of watching me at work'. But, soon enough, the tomcats seemed to select her choicest plant, get on either side of it, then use their back legs to kick the specimen into oblivion. The Suffolk lady soon had recourse to that traditional New Zealand remedy: wire netting.

'Nothing good can be said of the wandering cat,' wrote Guthrie-Smith in his magisterial tome on farm life in Hawke's Bay, *Tutira* (1921): 'The evil wrought by the roaming brutes outweighs by far the good.' He noted, with satisfaction, that during a storm when eleven 'half drowned animals' crowded into the men's quarters and cook-shop they were summarily caught and shot.

Yet if one searches through the photographs held at the Alexander Turnbull Library one comes upon another story. A lone gumdigger sits nursing a kitten. The man is old, lonely and far away from everything familiar. The tiny kitten gives him comfort and affection. In France, during the hell of the First World War, New Zealand diggers take time off to frolic with a cat. They play games with it. For a moment they return to another — more domestic — universe. Jean Batten gets off her plane in triumph: in her hands this eccentric pioneer holds a tiny black kitten. Has it been on her epochal flight?

The cat, the kitten has always been kind in offering comfort to strangers. When Samuel Butler, a man who never married, came to New Zealand in 1859, what else but a cat would upholster his solitude? Cats came with houses, fires, food. They required only a warm knee and a few kind words — and, of course, the scraps. In return they would offer an entire universe captured in the cat's observing eye.

In gathering together contributions for this book I have

turned to New Zealand writers to give some sense of the cat observed and the cat as observer. The cat has long had a privileged relationship with writers. Perhaps it is the cat's solitary nature or its ability to radiate a kind of silence and peacefulness that make it a particular favourite of writers. Or, I should say, *some* writers. When I was asking writers for contributions to this book I was sometimes met with a blank stare, and even a few incredulous glances.

It is all too easy for a book on pets, and cats in particular, to degenerate into a kind of terminal cuteness. My aim with this book has been to mine a rich seam in New Zealand writing that has seen the cat as friend, companion, muse. I couldn't persuade an author who suffers from asthma to write about the way a cat always zeroes in on the person least comfortable with its presence. Nor could I coax out those martinets who regard cats as beings whose one aim in life is to perform acts of politically incorrect destruction on our vulnerable native birdlife. This is particularly disappointing, as it is a widely held view among people who dislike cats. Instead I have some very touching stories, memoirs and poems. In fact, I must admit to being surprised at the number of poems about cats. This set me wondering whether there was some particular relationship between the poem — often a philosophical musing put with extraordinary nicety — and an animal that is famous for its fastidiousness. And even when the poems are caustic or even brutal, as in Bernard Brown's ditty, the cat and the poem seem suited to each other, a brief form of salute. But for every salute there is also a quiver of uneasiness.

Cats have been seen as carriers of evil spirits from medieval times. Of course, before that they had been deities:

both attitudes seem to presume a form of awesome power, perhaps based on the cat's preference for independence, their inscrutability, their harvesting of silence. It would seem to me that this relationship of a cat to silence suits a writer most of all. A cat does not need walking or watering, nor does a wet nose come and lay itself, imploringly, against your knee. As Martin Edmond astutely comments, his cat, Monkey, sat watching him as he wrote, as if to 'keep him honest'.

In Frank Sargeson's coruscating story 'Sale Day', we go back to the starkness of Guthrie-Smith's world of roaming brutes: the cat is an agent of the devil or its close cousin, sexuality. But then we move on to the lovely trio of poems by the gardener Ursula Bethell, where the cat is companion and muse. Beside them we have a grunty poem by that smelly old tom, James K. Baxter. In some ways these poems, stories and essays about cats could be mirrors into psyches, or subtle self-portraits. We read into animals the sentences we might like to murmur about ourselves. In this way a cat can be all things to all people: hostile enemy, stalker, evil spirit or most-loved mog. The memoirs in this book seem particularly strong, possibly for this reason. Dame Fiona Kidman reflects on the cats that have passed through her life, talking about a pair of cats who echoed the enmity of two of her maiden aunts; Shonagh Koea writes poignantly about how the white Manx Small 'saved my life'. Beryl Fletcher's 'Cat as Memoir' sums up the energy of people writing about animals that they unguardedly love. Barbara Else talks about the difficult business of burying a beloved cat, while Douglas Wright touches lightly but profoundly on the moral universe of humans and their animals.

The nature of a writer living with a cat is exquisitely glimpsed in Katherine Mansfield's intimate, charming relationship with her female cat, Charlie Chaplin. A woman alone in a foreign country, suffering a terminal illness, Mansfield had a peculiarly intense yet playful relationship with her cat. She provided an imaginary family tree for Charlie's kittens and brought all her formidable talents to bear in illuminating the character of her companion. Some people might have said that Mansfield, a famously catty woman, at times the complete bitch, could be expected to have an affinity with such a cruel animal. There is certainly a sense of sheathed claws with Mansfield. Yet her writing about Wingley is Mansfield at her best: lyrical, unguarded, intensely present. And comic. This ability to make an animal come to life is mirrored in another famous New Zealand *femme seule*, the painter Frances Hodgkins. To her we owe the extraordinarily charming, acutely observed drawings of a cat that featured in her life, called, tongue in cheek, 'The Black Devil'.

In one way, I suppose, the relationship between a cat and a person who lives on their own highlights one of the special relationships of cat to human. For a long time the cat has offered a special healing grace for the isolate. With a cat, one is never alone. Yet cats have also taken their place in family environments: many of the writers here trace the declension of cats through families that expand and contract. For this reason I have included some stories in which cats make only a momentary appearance, like Vivienne Plumb's prose poem 'The Cinematic Experience' and Sarah Quigley's short story 'Q: So Where Do all the Cicadas Go?' I make no apology for this, as it is in the nature of a cat to coil into a room, then slither out like a shadow, leaving behind a changed atmosphere. As

Vivienne Plumb implies, a cat's presence in a story, or a film, or a poem is never accidental. A cat has too much presence for that.

And peppered throughout these pieces of writing are some very astute comments on this most enigmatic of animals. Whether there is anything especially local about these comments I leave it up to the reader to decide.

Many a time have I beheld his little merriments with delight,
and his superior intelligence with surprise:
Never will his like be seen again!

Matthew Flinders

I hope this book gives cat lovers the pleasures of recognition, the comfort in knowing others are as besotted with these small animals, and that the poems, stories and essays give pleasure where pleasure is due: ladies and gentlemen, boys and girls — the cat!

Peter Wells

poems

HONE TUWHARE

Kitten

the phone didn't ring
yesterday.

it never even looked like
starting

and no letters've come
today, either — except

a stray kitten

i have given it milk;
it has adopted me

we've had a brief talk
about his mum? his dad?

you might say it was
a one-sided chat about cats:

but nothing's come of it

kitten knows only two
words and one of them is:

slurp

it is making love to my
feet: it understands

my loneliness . . . miaow?

PAULA GREEN

Blessing in Disguise

Our house is a cat magnet,
a soft touch in the neighbourhood
for every feline exile finding sanctuary
amidst the pool of words and paint.

Charlie, the longhaired domestic
slunk in to the nostalgic beat
of subterranean homesick blues
set to make a collage of the past

and future. He chewed through the TV
guide but left us Rialto and MGM.
He gnawed the *Dominion Post*
leaving 'Aotearoa Cloud', the Friday poem

a silver lining across our floor, as if
his grey fur weren't enough.

EMMA NEALE

Familiar

The cat comes inside,
scent of wood smoke in his fur
black coat beaded with cold
as the sky is with stars.
One ear is nicked,
devilishly cloven by an old fight.
There are strands in his tail
the grey of close calls
but he's a keg of a cat:
laughter drinks from him.
Often we ask what he thinks of the situation:
he winks, but he's got his own tongue.

Brute Instinct

For R. R.

The way an injured cat crawls forward when you call
its eyes in high-green fever
tail stripped right to the skin, a thin wet whip
so you have to tighten back sick at the sight

to cry out its stupid, human name
and the way, left with one blunt inch of stump,
hindquarters anaesthetised and numb,
still it jumps and stumbles to your lap

makes you think, odd enough, of those early talks
of trust:

nights curled close in to his ribs
like a fruit fitted with its one smooth pip

until he said it's stifling to be needed
don't need me so much

and of how now you'd agree
it's terrible
but not the need, the courage
in what he called
your dumb, animal love.

Fever

The snores of the cat, the child, the fire:
a three-toned clock
that times an afternoon calm

after the child's night fever, the dawn killing of a bird
that left the house adrift in shadow
that swirled and boiled as soon as we breathed:
a spring frost of black feathers
the bird's red heart
still at the centre
of the crude museum of flight.

Woken early, the child stood snared in the smudgy web
distraught over how now to love both bird and cat —
cried herself into cooler sleep
as if blood, beak, dark, dry snow
were all a last lurch of fever.

She dozes now
where the cat curls
safe on the couch
danger retracted like a claw,
and the grey sky outside
might still be crossed
by the fleet rocket
of a songbird.

As we watch her fitful rest —
the cat's green dragon eye
closed behind its eyelid,
the flower of mercury drawn down
into its thin glass bulb,
the flame sucked back
into the lung of an unlit match —
our bodies conceal night, knowledge, loss.

VINCENT O'SULLIVAN

The Cat on the Mat and the Man Watching

The man who envies the cat he looks at
sprawled on a ginger rug with her several
tones of greyness, the ripple of breath
beneath the high indifference of such comforting
sunlight, might very well call her
'Madame' for all he perceives of cat.
He is watching complacent symbol,
the cat on the mat mere feline mirror. He thinks
'How unhappy is man, that glutted
sensorium, that bible with its pages
ripped.' (Or such things as those.)
Thus the cat is quite filched from where
nature set it. Mere contrast to man
defuses cat completely.
    That man on another
day, his feet edging the rug,
while the same or another cat cadges
attention, humps for the stroking palm
or the chucked slop, despises oh
how completely that servile purr!
Superior thus from his angle
of the human at ease, the sun worn
as by right and the promises, promises
of evening, night, next week, a lifetime. He rolls on his own rug
in an image he'd disdain. He too
in the moment's sunlight, believing it his.

cats I have known

PETER BLAND

Cats I Have Known

I was going to call this recollection 'Cats I have owned', but of course no one owns a cat. You simply share their existence. Often they walk into your life out of their own need. *They* choose you.

I've moved around quite a lot and usually felt too unsettled to offer any animal a home. It wouldn't be fair. Cats, like children, need routine, stability, and the chance to develop a strong sense of territory. True, but the lack of these has never been a deterrent to their arrival. For a dumped or sick moggy, food and warmth come first. The rest is just a matter of time.

Anyway, wherever I've lived, I've no sooner unpacked and brewed my first pot of tea before a cat turns up to investigate the new arrivals.

Mostly they're sick, starving, or obviously lost. They'll slink around for a few hours waiting for their first saucer of milk, pretending to be untouchable, feigning a total distrust that hints at former cruelties . . . but, within a few days, they're on your lap purring like a Bentley.

There's a touch of Zen in these feline appearances. A sense that they know more than they're letting on, that they somehow slink effortlessly between parallel universes; so that their mythical nine lives are more a matter of inhabiting different realities than simply staying alive.

In our family we've had white cats, black cats, tabbies, Persians, and the odd semi-feral, happy to be fed but not handled . . . distant, savage, and sly. Some cats were simply passing through. Others were well-established neighbours' pets who put us at the top of their visiting list, good for a dribbling tickle or the odd scrap of meat but acceptable only on *their* terms and annoyingly arrogant when faced by a locked door.

I watched a cat die once. It staggered into the kitchen, a total stranger, frozen with cat flu. We made it as comfortable as possible and stroked it gently as it breathed its last. It did not go gentle into that good night but sank its teeth into my thumb and hung on grimly as the light faded from its eyes.

One favourite cat comes to mind. A black-and-white female we called Tao turned up with a huge abcess in her side. We got her treated and she became a well-loved part of our lives for the next seven years. Eventually we moved overseas and Tao went to my daughter's house just down the road. She always seemed to be waiting when I returned to New Zealand on holiday, and appeared from nowhere as soon as I was within fifty yards of the house. There was an uncanny bonding between us that seemed to ignore both time and space but which, on an instinctive level, seemed totally natural. When, in my absence, she was run over, I felt her loss deeply, as though I'd somehow let her down . . . that, in some primal sense, she'd been 'a familiar', not properly appreciated for the many elusive mysteries of her presence.

When my children were very young and we were living in a shack at Pukerua Bay, a white cat we called Mishi turned up to save us from a plague of rats. Although she was almost deaf she was a superb hunter, leaving the remains of her nightly catch

— head, tail and feet — outside the front door every morning. She developed skin cancer on her ears and had to have them cut back and covered in purple dye. She looked like a small polar bear with blunt blue horns. Being earless didn't affect her talents as a hunter but, one day, she was run over trying to cross a busy road. The children were heartbroken, the rats returned, and her absence haunted us for years.

New cats quickly arrive from nowhere to inhabit the spaces where older cats have been. Even as I write this, a next-door Persian called Dusty has included us in his territory. He paws at the window or curls up on the piano stool. He's beautiful, intelligent, sneaky and restless, but he'll never be a Tao or a Mishi. There's a special bonding when a cat finds you out and wants to belong, a sense of privilege and shared adventure.

KATHERINE MANSFIELD

Letter Extracts

From letter to Virginia Woolf
[April 1919]

On April 5th our one daffodil came into flower and our cat, Charlie Chaplin, had a kitten.

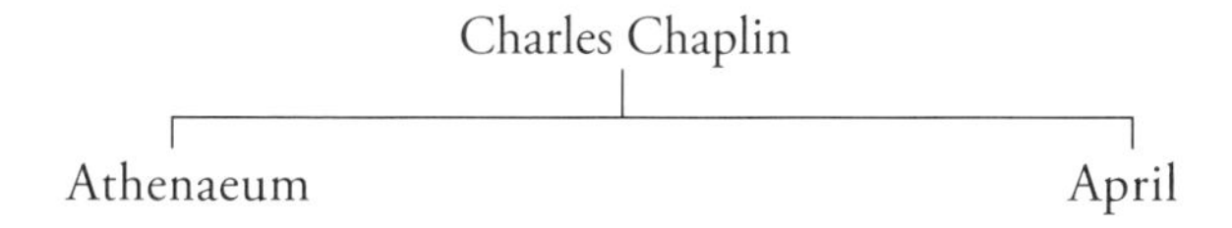

Athenaeum is like a prehistoric lizard, in very little. He emerged very strangely — as though hurtling through space flung by the indignant Lord. I attended the birth. Charles implored me. He behaved so strangely: he became a beautiful, tragic figure with blue-green eyes, terrified and wild. He would only lie still when I stroked his belly and said, 'It's all right, old chap. It's bound to happen to a man sooner or later.' And, in the middle of his pangs, his betrayer, a wretch of a cat with a face like a penny bun and the cat-equivalent of a brown bowler hat, rather rakish over one ear, began to *howl* from outside. 'Fool that I have been!' said Charles, grinding his claws against my sleeve. The second kitten, April, was born during the night, a snug, compact little girl. When she sucks she looks like a small infant saying its prayers and *knowing* that Jesus loves her. They are both loves; their paws inside are very soft, very pink, just like unripe raspberries . . .

From letter to the Hon. Dorothy Brett
[September 1921]

You know Wingley? The Mountain* brought him over. He arrived with immense eyes after having flown through all that landscape and it was several hours before the famous purr came into action. Now he's completely settled down and reads Shakespeare with us in the evenings. I wonder what cat-Shakespeare is like? We expect him to write his reminiscences shortly. They are to be bound in mouse-skin . . .

From letter to the Hon. Dorothy Brett
[12 November 1921]

The Fat Cat sits on my Feet.

Fat is not the word to describe him by now. He must weigh pounds and pounds. And his lovely black coat is turning white. I suppose it's to prevent the mountains from seeing him. He sleeps here and occasionally creeps up to my chest and pads softly with his paws, singing the while. I suppose he wants to see if I have the same face all night. I long to surprise him with terrific disguises.

M. calls him 'My *Breakfast* Cat' because they share that meal, M. *at* the table and Wingley *on*. It's awful the love one can lavish on an animal.

* Ida Baker, Katherine Mansfield's great friend

MARTIN EDMOND

Monkey

It was 1983. An evening in spring. We were going out to eat at a Cambodian restaurant in Glebe Point Road where the chef was a former diplomat who fled the massacres orchestrated by Pol Pot. As we passed by the head of an alley that runs behind the Glebe Post Office, a small bundle of tortoiseshell fur hurtled across our path, squalling: yeeeoowww . . . yeeeoooowww . . . ! The cries were intense, pleading, desperate. I looked down and saw that the membranes which slide out from the corners of cats' eyes were swollen, yellow, mucous-stained, all but obscuring her sight. She was half grown, skinny, malnourished. And she would not stop crying and snaking around my ankles.

I went around to a shop on the main drag and bought a can of cat food and a small container of milk before realising it wasn't really practical to feed her on the street without a dish or a spoon. Or a can opener. We decided to take her home and feed her there. Although she did not seem like a cat who'd been handled much, she lay quietly against my chest as we walked back down the hill and up again into Darghan Street. Our building was on old sea cliffs at the very end of the road, looking out over Blackwattle Bay. It was a ground-floor flat with a back entrance through an open concreted area. This was where I dished out a plate of cat food, poured a saucer of milk; she gobbled the one at scarcely believable speed and ignored the other completely. She never did drink milk.

If you're still here when we get back from the restaurant, I said, *you can stay.* I thought she might wander off to her old haunts once she'd eaten; but she didn't. Some compact had been struck between us. She was there when we returned and there she stayed. What's more, from that night forth she regarded me as her friend, her protector, almost her possession. Nothing could shake her feeling that I belonged to her, and she to me. It was a loyalty of dog-like proportions.

I doubt she'd ever been in a flat, because she regarded the ceilings with outright suspicion. They were coated with nasty stuff called vermiculite, a grey, friable material, probably sprayed on; but it wasn't that that made her leery: I think she saw it as a different kind of sky, more oppressive and threatening than those she was used to. She'd certainly never been to a vet before, nor in a box either. I gave up trying to confine her and just carried her in my arms. The cocktail of smells in the waiting room filled her with terror and she dug her claws into me, trying to climb to some higher point of safety, like the top of my head. Somehow we held her still long enough for the jabs; then I carried her home again.

My partner at the time took to calling her *You little monkey* and one day when a friend, who was Chinese, was visiting, she heard this and said thoughtfully: *Yes, she does look like a monkey.* So that's what we called her. I guess there were associations with the sagacious and infinitely inventive Monkey of Chinese legend but in another way it was just a name that fitted. She had a curiously quatrefoil face, divided down the nose, half black and half ginger, with the colours repeated in reverse in the soft fur under her chin; lower down there was a little bib of white and she also had a white tip to her tail. Otherwise, she was a classic short-haired tortoiseshell.

When her health recovered, which it did remarkably quickly, Monkey went out and got pregnant. She had four kittens in the wardrobe of our bedroom: a marmalade tom, a grey female with subtle patches of white and ginger, and two tortoiseshells much like herself, one of which was stillborn. Motherhood was a shock to her. She could hardly bear to leave her kittens even for a moment and when hunger or the need to go outside became too great, she would race madly through the flat on her way to the plates in the kitchen or else out the laundry window to relieve herself; and then race back. She seemed to think her kittens might disappear if she wasn't there with them.

When, in due course, they grew up, we had Monkey spayed, gave the ginger tom and the grey away, and kept the tortoiseshell. She turned out bigger and healthier than her mother, and much dumber. We called her Puzzle because that's what so much of life seemed to be for her. She could not, for instance, when young, work out how to walk along the ranch slider to the gap where it was left open to the small balcony of the flat and instead, while her brother and sister sported outside, paddled plaintively at the glass as if it might somehow thereby open for her. Once she had weaned her, Monkey regarded Puzzle with the same suspicion she extended to all other cats. She tolerated her, but she didn't much like her, hissing if she came too close.

For Monkey was a loner. The only person she really trusted was me. You could see this when people came around. They would exclaim, as people will over a pretty cat, and start to stroke her. She'd accept the first stroke, endure the second and on the third, most often, snarl and bite the hand that petted her. She was a biter by nature: she'd often bite me, but delicately, never once drawing blood. I took these nips as marks of affection. We also used to have play fights during which her eyes would go mad and dark and she would rear up on her haunches, slashing at me with her claws; but she never deliberately hurt me.

She stayed wild in other ways. Outside our flat there was a railway line, used intermittently by goods trains, and on ledges within the road and pedestrian tunnels that passed beneath the tracks, pigeons roosted. Despite the fact that she was fed regularly, Monkey liked to go down to the railway line and hunt. She'd bring the pigeons back in her mouth and dismember them in the small triangular garden next to the balcony. Gradually it filled up with feathers, beaks and claws. The rest of the bird, she'd eat.

She had other wild ways. I have a full-head mask of Anubis I made for the 1978 Red Mole show *Ghost Rite*. One day, after this mask was used in a photo shoot for a rock band, it was left upright on the sitting-room floor beside the television. When Monkey came in and saw it, all the fur on her body stood up on end and she began to walk, stiff-legged, incredibly slowly, sideways away from it. I had to hide the mask after that; if she even glimpsed it, she behaved in that same way — as if the Egyptian jackal-god of the dead had indeed come down among us. I took this as a compliment to my rather average mask-making abilities.

When my relationship ended and I moved out of the flat, Monkey moved out too. I don't mean she came with me; I went to live in some squats where it simply wasn't possible for her to be — there was too much other feral life around — so she went down on the railway line with her pigeons. She'd come back to the flat to be fed, but that was all. If I wanted to see her, I'd go down into the wasteland of long grass and weeds that flanked the rails and whistle — a long, quavering warble that made her come bounding like a miniature cheetah through the grass towards me from wherever it was she had her lair. We kept our connection going this way for about nine months, until I found a flat where she could live and we were reunited. I'm quite sure she was relieved that she no longer had to see her daughter Puzzle, not even for a moment.

The new flat was on the second floor so there was no way she could have her own window entrance as she had in Darghan Street. A cat door wasn't possible either. I never left her inside when I went out and I never found out where she went when I wasn't around. When I returned by car she'd recognise the sound of the motor and appear, slinking along close to the ground until she was near enough to feel safe, at which point the flag of her tail would be raised. If I was on foot, the same ineluctable sensors informed her that I was back and, either way, she would bound up the tiled stairs to the flat beside me. While I was working she would sit on the desk watching, with a faintly admonitory look in her green eyes, as if keeping me honest. On the rare occasions she deigned to sit in my lap, I took it as a great honour. At night, she would sleep on the end of the bed near my feet, curled into the tightest ball I've ever known a cat to make, like a coil of knotted, black-and-tan rope.

In those days I had friends living at a place called Tinda

Creek on the Putty Road, which runs from northwestern Sydney along the eastern flank of the Blue Mountains, north to the Hunter Valley. Their house was about a kilometre off the highway, surrounded by bush in which both native wildlife and feral humans lurked. I took Monkey out there one Christmas. My friends had a cat too, a big, languid tabby called Squeaky. Monkey couldn't even begin to handle the possibility of spending time confined in a strange place with another cat and, the first chance she got, took off. We didn't find her for days, though we called and called. It wasn't until just before I left to go back to town that she was discovered, holed up in a thicket about fifty metres from the house. She must have spent the entire time in there, watching, waiting, listening to, smelling the strangeness of the Australian bush.

I moved again, to Darlinghurst, to a flat on the top storey of a terrace house with a cat flap extant in the kitchen door. There were many cats in Womerah Lane, and Monkey disliked all of them. She particularly disliked the way some of them used the cat flap to enter her domain. They'd hang around in the sitting room in the wee small hours, with Monkey muttering and growling from a high place somewhere. Her solution, as ever, was to make a lair for herself outside. She'd wait there for my return, just as she had in Glebe. When I bought a new car, she learned the sound of its motor too and would reliably appear as I rounded the corner into the laneway.

Monkey's health wasn't good. Her coat never really attained the glossy sheen of real contentment. When stressed, which she often was, she was in the habit of pulling out the fur along her back and usually had bald patches towards her tail. Trying to treat her for flea infestation, which does cause some cats to pull out their fur, was difficult if not impossible. She would never allow herself to be bathed, she hated flea collars, she wouldn't take pills administered by hand and wouldn't touch food with ground-up tablets in it. In the end I gave up and let her be. She was also quite a greedy cat, though never fat. She tended to eat too much and then vomit, like a Roman, from sheer overindulgence. This too I put down to her blighted, hungry youth.

After about a year in Darlinghurst I began living with someone again; she had a cat of her own, another stray, but of a rather different kind than Monkey. Coco (after Coco Chanel) was a pedigree chocolate Burmese who we thought was probably mistreated by his yuppie owners and had run away. He was as fanatically loyal to his owner as Monkey was to me. Of course Monkey hated Coco; but after a while a funny thing happened. Coco decided to stake out a piece of territory that the neighbourhood cats would respect. It took him about a year and included a series of epic encounters with one particular moggy we knew only as *the black cat*, but in the end he managed it. Our flat, the sometime midnight rendezvous point for various cat festivities convened while we were sleeping, became the sole preserve of Monkey and Coco.

After that, Monkey decided she would put up with Coco, even if she never became actively affectionate towards him. Sometimes when they were both on the bed they would inadvertently end up curled back to back with just their rumps touching. Sometimes they would find themselves sprawled companionably together in front of the Conray heater. It was hilarious to watch Monkey wake up and discover she had been, as it were, sleeping with Coco. Her dignity offended, she would hiss, edge warily away and then start frantically grooming; while Coco just blinked lazy golden eyes at her. The two strays shared one other habit: Coco, though rather more amenable to treatment for fleas, was also an inveterate puller-out of his hair. When the fur flew between this odd couple, all wounds were self-inflicted.

After twelve years together, Monkey vanished from my life in the same enigmatic fashion she arrived. In 1995 the house in Womerah Lane was sold and we decided to move to the outskirts of Sydney. We found a place but, between leaving Womerah and going to Pearl Beach, took a six-week holiday in New Zealand. I left Monkey with a friend in Paddington. During those six weeks, my friend fell in love with a woman who lived in Penrith, on the far western fringes of the metropolis, a good two hours' drive away. Somehow, during those days and nights when he was absent, Monkey lost faith. She disappeared. When I returned I combed the neighbourhood, whistling her whistle, for hours on end, but I never found her.

It hurts me to think that I betrayed the compact we had, that I let her down, let her go. On the other hand, I wouldn't be surprised if she found someone else to look after her, some old lady perhaps. Even in the early days in Glebe she was one of those cats who have several people feeding them, as I discovered one evening down by the railway line when I came upon her tucking into a plate of Snappy Tom someone had put out for her. She finished it off before greeting me. She always did have her priorities.

I miss her still. I miss her quack *Hello*, her wise advice, her simple presence. I've not had another cat since. But recently

I encountered a couple eerily similar to Monkey and Puzzle both in looks and personality, except these two got on with each other and the daughter wasn't quite as dumb as Puzzle. They recalled an old superstition: that there is only a certain number of cat souls in the world and hence every cat is a reincarnation of another cat; for no new cat can be born until an old one dies. In this way, it is said, every cat is as Egyptian as the first cats were. Which means, perhaps, that somewhere out in the world, the soul of Monkey inhabits another cat body: querulous, cantankerous, loyal, spooky and spooked, she'll be in close compact with another human, one she adores in the same way she adored me; and, I trust, s/he her.

Barbara Else

Alcatraz: Marital Property

I nearly didn't choose him because he had a dirty bib. Seventeen years later, in a corner of my fernery, I tacked up a small brass plaque: *Alcatraz, 1998 — a verray parfit gentil catte.* He was the cat of my life.

In 1980 my first husband and I, with our daughters, returned to New Zealand after three years in San Diego. We'd promised the girls that once we had bought a house we'd have animals, animals, animals. As so often happens with big promises, it came down to one cat. We all went to choose her from the SPCA. Jim named her Enchilada to note our Californian experience — she was a tortoiseshell and looked as though she were covered in cheese. She was a dreadful cat, possibly because we had her spayed in the middle of her first season: *Yow-rr, yow-rrr . . .* 'Dad,' asked 11-year-old Emma, '— is she crying because it is a need or a longing?' (Good question. Any answers, let me know.) Enchilada persistently leapt into a shrub Jim planted near the back door and reshaped it to make a bowl-shaped toilet. She also used his study as a toilet, far under the desk in the dark. We had to get rid of her. 'No more cats,' said Jim, and went back overseas for a research trip of several months.

The girls were at school all day. I sat and wrote, or read, and tended house. I did small research tasks for Jim. The house was big and empty.

I am a stubborn soul. I returned to the SPCA all by myself. There were many, many cats to choose from, some actively pleading, some depressed, some old, some far too young. In one cage was a fluffy black-and-white male who looked at me with a resigned appeal. He had a grubby spot on his white chest. I walked on. But I turned to look again and eventually decided the mark was part of his fur — it wasn't that he couldn't clean himself.

As I drove him home, it felt like springing him from prison. So the perfect name was Alcatraz. A name with many connotations, I thought, which could nicely shorten to 'Trazzy'.

The girls were delighted with this 12-month-old ball of fluff and scurry. 'Alky!' they called. 'Here, Alky!' I had to admit the nickname had more bite than the over-cute one I'd come up with. The grubby mark was dirt, and soon disappeared. He turned out to be fastidious with his smart suit.

In those first few days Alcatraz made just one social bloop, very neatly on Jim's side of the marital bed. I took that as a clever critical comment, washed the bedspread and told nobody.

By the time Jim arrived home, Alcatraz was a fixture in my life. Over the next few years, he sat near me while I wrote. He played in the garden when I was out there, nearly losing a paw several times when I pruned hydrangeas and flowering currant. He battled Clerp, the neighbour's ex-farm cat whom he loathed, and left tufts of Clerp blowing in the brisk Karori wind.

If I took the bus into town, Alcatraz trailed after me to the bus stop and looked offended as I rode away. He followed my youngest, Sarah, to school on a regular basis, to sit staring into her classroom till her teacher told her to 'take your cat home *again*'. For some months he disappeared each day and trudged back across the road at dinner time. He'd been sitting outside a neighbour's aviary from nine to five — just watching.

He never learned that you couldn't get in if you flung yourself the half-open bedroom window. Many summer nights I woke hearing the crash of a furry body against the glass, a crunch as he toppled backwards on the gravel. I could picture his bruised pride.

He had his own song: all my cats seem to have a song, which I discover and sing to them once they've lived with me for a while. His refrain was: 'my Alley Cat razz-a-ma-tazz.' He suffered it and my dancing with him in a gentlemanlike manner.

In 1988, the marriage broke up. When it came to dividing the property, it was done through lawyers. I've thrown out the papers dealing with it all — too painful to hold onto them. But I remember giving my lawyer a list of what I wanted with something like a P.S. at the foot: 'And I would like to have Alcatraz. If you agree to this, can I also have the stool that he scratches?'

It was a rectangular footstool I'd once given Jim for a birthday present ($18.95 still written on the base), reupholstered twice because it turned out to be a perfect claw-exerciser. I still have it, and have given it two further claw-friendly covers.

Sarah tells me she cried and cried when Alky left. He was, of course, a symbol of the marriage and its ending. I still wish I could have taken Sarah too and I cry inside myself, to think about those times. But I had my old love Alcatraz again and I had my new love, Chris. For some months, Alky seemed frightened of large male feet, though only when Chris wore shoes. Soon enough he deigned to accept Chris as an acceptable co-owner.

Our home was surrounded with trees. Alky knew each one up to the twiglets. We had a pole house, and he also climbed the poles inside to sit like a gargoyle in the gap below the living-room ceiling. From the side, he looked aristocratic, the Lion King. Full-face, he was a cartoon, Sylvester's double. He had a fine expression of wounded dignity if you laughed at him — he knew how beautiful he was. When Chris and I had our marriage ceremony in the garden on that warm, calm Wellington evening with a host of friends, Alky wore a cluster of coloured ribbons, posing for the guests, soaking up the company and admiration.

After my first novel was published, Jane Ussher came to photograph me for the *Listener*. She took a single glance around the room and pointed to the cat: 'He'll go on the back of the sofa. You stand there.' He had his photo in the *Listener* twice, my handsome boy.

As he grew old he began to show signs of depression whenever we had to leave him in a cattery. He became uraemic. By now he was eighteen, a good age for a cat, and winter was coming. I spoke to the vet, who agreed it was time to make the terrible decision. It had to be done before the weather turned too cold and wet, when poor Alcatraz would have been completely miserable. I wasn't going to take him to the surgery — he hated the vet's rooms far too much by now. It would be done at home in the garden.

I phoned the vet again to arrange it for just after Easter. Another vet answered. She was abrupt and said she could do it only that very afternoon. I had a lunch date with some friends and could hardly talk to them — their faces, as I left, were full of sympathy.

The afternoon was sunny. Smelly old Alcatraz, bone-thin and shaky, sat in the garden while I brushed him and told him what a handsome love he was. He purred for the first time in several weeks. When the vet came down the steps she seemed surprised to see him so glossy. Chris was there, ready to hold him, ready to hold me — but when the vet asked what we would prefer I managed to indicate wordlessly that I would hold him, that it would be done in our peaceful fernery. I sat with him on my lap, my handsome boy.

I watched him intently as he relaxed, rested on me, became so still, so still, stopped breathing. I held him. I held him.

The vet said: 'He was very sick — it was the right thing to do — I'm sorry if I rushed you.' I nodded, still unable to speak or take my eyes off Alcatraz. She hurried back up the steps and I remember thinking how appalling this part of her job must be.

I chose a pillowcase to wrap him in and Chris dug a hole at the foot of one of our most goodly trees. That weekend, we chose a hebe to mark the spot. 'He deserves a fine plaque too,' said Chris.

Indeed he did. I nailed it up in a discreet corner of the fernery, and there it might remain. My verray parfit gentil Alcatraz.

GRAEME LAY

Landing on Their Feet

As the flight from Tahiti began its descent into Auckland, I started to fill in the customs declaration card. As usual I had no firearms, my bag did not contain millions of dollars of currency and I carried no camping equipment. These 'No' boxes were firmly ticked. Then I came to the 'Food of any kind' section. Aware of the dire consequences should the food in my bag be undeclared but discovered, I ticked the 'Yes' box. The food was not fresh, but it was undeniably food: a three-pack of canned kitten food, bought the day before in a Papeete supermarket. That wouldn't cause any problems with MAF. It was to be a special treat for the two youngsters at home.

The phone call from Elsa, our local vet, had come just before Christmas. Did I still want a pair of kittens? An abandoned pair, about three weeks old, had been handed in to her practice. Both our aged cats — Gemma and Georgina — had had to be put down during the year, and a cat-lover's household without cats is a bereft one indeed. I told Elsa I'd come right down and check the foundlings out.

They were brother and sister, tiny tabbies, with bright-white legs and chests. The mottled, grey-and-black markings on their backs were startlingly beautiful, like the skin of a python. They were gorgeous, adorable, irresistible. The kittens' mother, probably a stray, solo parent overburdened with her lot, had left them under a house in Devonport. As the two kittens staggered to their feet and mewed at me beseechingly from the confines of their cage, longing to be free, I didn't hesitate. 'Yes, I'll have them.'

In just days they were part of the household. Bright blue-eyed, alert and energetic, they already knew what the kitty-litter box was for, seldom failing to put it to good use. (In that respect cats are years ahead of humans, while dogs, those disgusting creatures, never learn.) Endlessly entertaining, they played with each other for hours, tumbling and leaping and chasing and hiding and seeking and stalking their feathery toys, before they suddenly and inexplicably stopped and fell asleep, curled into balls, tails wrapped around their tiny bodies like furry string. We named them Pippy and Jimmy. The orphaned kittens had, you might say, landed on their feet.

I became a fretting parent all over again. I nailed chicken wire around the deck, built gates over every possible escape route and kept all the windows firmly shut, in spite of the summer heat. I bought special-formula milk and sachets of kitten food from the vet's and mashed it up for them, just refraining from tasting it myself. I made elastic leashes and tied them to the flea collars, so that when they did go outside, their movements could be closely controlled. When they caught their first weta and brought it inside, I was prouder than they were.

And from the beginning, they showed that although their minds were tiny, they were very much their own. The old saying 'dogs have masters, cats have staff' sprang to mind. They played when they wanted to play, they ate when they wanted to eat, and not before. Tractable they weren't. Pippy proved particularly elusive, moving like lightning when she wasn't in a mood to be picked up. Adept at finding tiny crevices to crawl into and go to sleep, she liked entering the drawers of my writing desk from the back and snoozing with her head on a pile of floppy disks or boxes of transparencies.

Then, one evening just before Christmas, with Jimmy soundly asleep on a chair, Pippy disappeared. She was there one second, gone the next. We called, we searched, we notified the neighbours. All to no avail. As darkness fell, she still hadn't been found. I was beside myself. She had fallen into the creek and drowned, she had been devoured by the monstrous dog next door, she had been kidnapped for her lovely pelt.

I did yet another a cat-scan — searching every cupboard and wardrobe, the fireplaces, under every bed — but she had vanished. Stricken with grief, I began to design a 'Lost Kitten' poster on the computer, offering a huge reward. I would hand-deliver the poster to every household in Devonport. Yet I knew it was hopeless. She was so tiny, so vulnerable, so desirable.

Then, just as I was putting the finishing touches to the poster, I heard a faint sound. Was it a mewling? I turned around. In the office was a trundle bed. But I had already looked under its pillow and cover, several times. I went back to my computer. Then I heard it again. It *was* a tiny kitten's cry. I went to the bed, pulled out one of the drawers underneath it. And there was Pippy, peering up at me from one corner of the drawer, a little furry ball among the underwear. My relief was indescribable.

Then, on Christmas Day, Jimmy developed diarrhoea. Staggering about, visibly weak and deteriorating quickly, the little chap began to pass blood. A phone call to the emergency vet confirmed that it was serious: 'Get him here quickly, or you'll have a dead kitten by nightfall'. Jimmy spent two nights on antibiotics and being fed intravenously. When I collected him from the clinic, and saw his miraculous recovery, the only thing that stopped me embracing the vet was the fact that he was Greg.

So, given this besottedness on my part, it was predictable that as I cruised the aisles of a chic supermarket in Papeete, I should pause at the pet-food shelves and seek out the kitten section. Not just gourmet kitten-food, but *French* gourmet kitten-food. Nothing was too good for Jimmy and Pippy. And there it was, in 195-gram tins with orange labels: *Champion. Terrine. Pour chaton. Replas complet. Aliment complet.* Its '*vitamines*' were listed — A, D_3 and E. I bought a three-pack. The perfect overseas gift for the darlings.

At Auckland airport I collected my bag and joined the Red queue. Studying my declaration card, the young MAF woman asked, 'What food is it you have with you?'

'Kitten food. In tins,' I replied. She looked puzzled for a moment, then said, 'Join Queue C. The one over there.'

Queue C was long, and slow. Ahead of me, people of all races and nationalities were tearing open their cases and rummaging among their personal belongings, extracting packets and tins and sachets. At the head of the queue was a long bench, behind which uniformed people were scrutinising and frowning and picking at declared-and-suspect foodstuffs. I took out Jimmy and Pippy's three-pack, irritated now at the delay this was going to cause. The food had been cooked, it was in *tins*, for Christ's sake. How could it *possibly* be a threat to the nation's agricultural sector? Then I told myself, be patient, when they see that the food's in tins, they'll wave you through.

Alongside me were piles of clothing and other personal items and anxious-looking foreign people. Many looked disgruntled. 'Lois and Rodney will be wondering where on *earth* we are,' the man next to me, an upper-crust Englishman in tweeds, murmured to his wife. 'It's only *butterscotch*, after all.'

The queue crept forward, and in twenty minutes I was brought before the bench. My inquisitor was a man in his early forties, with black, close-cropped hair and a genial expression. He was wearing rubber gloves. When I handed the declaration card and the three-pack to him, his face darkened. 'What's this?' he asked. His voice was accented. South African perhaps.

'Kitten food.'

'*Kitten food*?'

'Yes.'

'Where from?'

'Tahiti. But originally from France. See, there. It says "Fabrique en France".' Unable to resist, I added, 'That means "Made in France".'

Holding the three-pack, looking at it with unallayed suspicion, the man said to the young woman next to him, 'France is a member of the EU, isn't it?'

'I think so,' she replied. It was impossible to tell whether or not this was helpful to my cause.

The man rotated one of the cans in his hand, squinting at

the label. His expression was now bordering on the hostile. '*Kitten food . . .*'

'It's been cooked. And, obviously, canned,' I said, trying to remain patient. It was very hot in the hall, my bag had to be repacked, and I hadn't even reached the X-ray machine yet. The man was shaking his head, holding the cans as if they were primed grenades.

'I'll have to take this away. For further examination.' He looked at me through narrowed eyes. 'Wait there.' And he disappeared through a door behind the bench.

I walked away and sat down on my bag. The tweedy Englishman and his wife strode past, pushing their trolley. '*Butterscotch*,' muttered the man. 'You'd think I was bringing in anthrax.' His wife giggled, nervously.

Ten, twenty minutes passed. The man had still not reappeared. I was about to flag it away and move on when I realised that he still had my declaration card. I couldn't leave the hall without handing it in. Then, at the half-hour mark, he reappeared, holding the three-pack. He looked around but at first couldn't see me. Angry by now, I called out to him. 'Over here!' Then I muttered, '*Nazi . . .*'

Handing over the cans, the official said airily, 'They've been X-rayed. They're okay, they're just kitten food.'

Back at home, it was left to my adult children to offer an explanation for the official's bellicose attitude.

'Drugs. He would have thought you had drugs in the cans.'

'Drugs?'

'Yes. Hard drugs. It would have been a pretty good cover,

wouldn't it? Kitten food. That's why he had them X-rayed.'

I shook my head at the strangeness of it all. Then I looked down at the kitchen floor, to where Jimmy and Pippy were tucking delightedly into their *Terrine pour chaton*. And smiled.

SHONAGH KOEA

Small

This is the story of my white Manx cat, Small, and of how she saved me.

Early in 1987 my husband, George Kingsford Koea, died very suddenly and unexpectedly. We had been packing up to go on holiday. An exhibition was being held then in Wellington of tomb figures, lifesize, from China. We often went away to Wellington or Auckland to art exhibitions because in New Plymouth where we lived the art exhibitions were always full of the same people and one grew tired of the same old faces. There would be the Thises and the Thats and the Something Elses and in the end it made you want to throw up. Small cities and towns are like that.

So we were packing up to go to Wellington to see these legendary tomb figures, whole armies in terracotta. George was a meticulous man who liked to leave everything immaculate. In the evening — and we were due to depart early the next day — we went out into the very large garden that surrounded the house we lived in then and we mowed the lawns at the front of the house. There was quite an imposing approach to the house with big, spreading trees — magnolias and rhododendrons, things like that — and George liked those lawns to be mowed with an old Morrison reel mower because it made stripes on the grass like you see on cricket fields. It used to look very beautiful. George was doing the actual mowing and I was taking away the clippings in a small wheelbarrow to spread, as a mulch, around the rhododendrons. There was a large Pink Pearl rhododendron at the side of the house and also a White Pearl and a Fragrantissima so I was spreading the clippings around those in turn and going back to the front lawn to get another load. I made several little trips but the last time I went back I thought it odd that the sound of the lawnmower was not retreating and advancing. It seemed to be coming from the same place. I found the mower roaring away beside a bed of very handsome pink gazanias in full flower and George lying dead among them.

His heart attack was sudden and unexpected and my life from that moment became horribly and remarkably different, like those diagrams you see in books sometimes of what Pompeii was like before and after the eruption of Vesuvius, or like Coventry Cathedral before and after the German bombers came over.

I became slowly and inexorably terrified because the change was so enormous and in many cases so grotesque. Men whom I had perceived, in my vague way, as the reasonably pleasant husbands of women I knew suddenly came and pinched my bottom. There were wrestling matches at the foot of the stairs. I ordered people out of the house. One of my son's schoolmasters appeared one evening and asked me when I was going upstairs to turn 'our' electric blanket on. People I had thought were friends came and said they had never liked my hair and something would have to be done about it now. I do not know why because my hair has always been the same and still is. A man came very persistently for several evenings wanting to take my grand piano away for a minimal price, out of the goodness of his heart, because he said I would not play it again. Another man called at the house many times wanting to remove all the furniture from the upstairs rooms, again because I would not want it any more.

The most extraordinary things happened and I became most deeply frightened. I became too frightened to even answer the doorbell. A couple I did not know (except by sight around the town) called so persistently that I strode through the entrance hall and unscrewed the back of the bell one day. It was going ring-ring-ring and suddenly just went scratch-scratch-scratch, which I thought was actually rather funny. There was a curious sort of little vantage point at the second bend in the staircase of whoever might be at the door. Often I used to see who was there and would think, 'Oh I don't know them — I can't be bothered being stared at any more.' People come and stare at you if your husband dies very suddenly and you are quite young, which I was then.

After the business of the people who came and rang the doorbell nine times and I never answered, the new editor of the newspaper — George had been the editor of the evening newspaper in New Plymouth — came up to the house very carefully to see how I was. The people had gone down to the office to report that I must be mad. It seemed to them incomprehensible that they would open my gates and drive all the way up to my house and ring the doorbell vigorously nine times and get no answer but, again, people in small places are like that. People in larger places would not have the time and there would be lots of other things, like murders and gangland rapes and vicious bank robberies, to harness morbid curiosity.

'Oh,' I said to the new editor, 'so this is a madness inspection, is it?' I had thought, when he arrived in the early evening, that it was just a pleasant visit. Memory plays tricks but I think I was standing beside the big fireplace in the sitting room, with the view down to the sea stretching away beyond the bay window, and I had lit the fire because winter had come deeply down by then. I would have been leaning against the big mantelpiece on one elbow and with one booted foot neatly on the floor and the other crossed at the ankle and resting on one toe. This seemingly casual but watchfully louche attitude was one I seemed to have taken up since George died and it in no way indicated relaxation. By then, too, I probably would have been wearing black jeans and a black jersey which had become, suddenly, my uniform and remains so. Being a kind of soldier in a hostile urban landscape was how I perceived the situation. The house was huge and glacial and all my jerseys had suddenly begun to wear out at once. Betrayed even by wool, I used to think, though this was probably the sort of fanciful notion a writer would get. Maybe the jerseys had been worn for long enough and they just happened to wear out then, during that particular winter.

My son was at medical school then, in Auckland, and he used to telephone me every Thursday evening from a pub, up the road from where he flatted in Ponsonby. They did not have a telephone in the flat. The sound of the telephone would echo through the house at the appointed time — we suddenly became a small family who used safe signals — and I would answer it. By then, when the telephone rang, I would mostly just stand in front of it watching it ring as one watches a performing animal in a circus. I never knew who it would be and it could have been one of the many callers who might say, 'Of course, my dear, I've never really liked you and I feel I should tell you now that you can't have all that hair. You've just got to have a haircut.' I found it endlessly puzzling.

By the following year I had become quite ill. Possibly, I think now, I had subconsciously tried to die by starving myself. I had not eaten very much for a long time because I always had such a big lump in my throat as if I was going to cry at any moment and it was difficult to swallow food. I used to mash bananas and mix them with wheatgerm and milk and eat that sludge because it would slip down easily, but my eating, overall, had been very inadequate since I found George dead in the garden.

I had not had much of a life before I met George so he was all the life and brightness I had ever had. Living without him was like living in the dark. I am explaining all this so anyone who reads it can understand how isolated I suddenly was and how lonely and frightened and can also understand how marvellous it was when I found the white Manx cat in the garden and she became my friend and ally, almost the only living creature I trusted.

At the time I became very sick it was high summer again, the anniversary of George's death I suppose. I mainly stayed upstairs in the house because going downstairs was too much of an effort. I used to wander down the three bends in the staircase to get myself bananas to eat. I tried to eat meat and things like that because I had become very anaemic, but it was all rather a half-hearted affair. Sometimes I used to walk through the downstairs part of the house and look into the dusty sitting room as if it belonged to someone else. The morning-room carpet was covered with a light dusting of dead slaters, belly-up, and I would open the door and say, 'Oh my God' to no one in particular and close the door again.

So that was how things were when, one day, I looked down onto the garden from an upstairs window and saw a small white animal hopping from one bush to another. The garden was very large and there were not a lot of flowerbeds. It was mostly just trees and shrubs and wide, irregular expanses of lawn. I thought the animal was a rabbit.

The following day I saw it again, making its devious little way, obviously watchful and nervous, from one bush to another. I went outside to investigate and discovered that the animal was a small white cat without a tail. At that stage I thought someone must have been very cruel to it and chopped off its tail and that was why it was so frightened. I found something for the little cat to eat and went out with the food on a saucer but the cat was very frightened and hid amid the greenery. I put down the saucer and went inside. Through the little leadlight window in the entrance hall, my great mainstay in detecting the approach of strangers, I watched and after a few minutes the little cat hopped out from its hiding place and ate the food.

We got into a kind of routine, the little cat and I. I would go outside and call, 'Come here, poor little small cat,' and the little cat would poke its head out of the bushes so I knew where it was. I would put down the food several yards away and go inside. After a while I took to crawling along on the lawn with the saucer held out and I was able to get closer and closer until one day I touched her very gently. Her fur was very thick. (Subsequently the local vet said she was an English Shorthair, whatever that might mean, with a double coat.)

There were eight neighbours where I lived then. The garden was very large and irregularly shaped so eight other properties bounded it at various places. Most of the neighbours I never knew because they were too far away. One family whose house was beside my drive was very kind. The man whose garden bounded my own towards the back suddenly claimed a large portion of my land and I had to call the police to get him out. My situation became extremely peculiar. Possibly such a large property occupied by one woman attracted attention. I do not know. One of the other neighbours, whose kitchen window slightly overlooked part of my front garden, came over one day and said darkly, 'Why don't you go away? Look you, we see you at night, walking around behind lit windows.' She was Welsh and a Welsh girl I got to know later said that in Wales the houses are mostly owned by the mining companies, or used to be, so that when a man dies his widow just disappears from the neighbourhood very rapidly because the house is needed for another miner. I found it very sad that I was not wanted but there was a curious dark humour in it too. When I crawled around the front lawn holding out a saucer of food to a funny little white tail-less cat hiding in the bushes and calling, 'Come here, poor little small cat,' the Welsh eyes at that kitchen window watched me calculatingly and I would say, as an aside to the cat, 'I'm in a bit of trouble there, you know, pussy.' The cat was already becoming my confidante.

In time I managed to coax her into the house, where she remained. She became what I called an inside cat. In time, too, I took her to the vet up the road to get an assessment of her needs and that was when I discovered, authoritatively, that she was a female, had never had a tail so was a Manx cat, and showed signs of severe injury. There had been, much earlier, some kind of severe blow to her hindquarters and lower spine, caused either by a car or a kick. This is what actually did for her in the end, though Small and I had a long way to go before that and we were always very happy.

Early in the year I found her in the garden I was in one of my stages of writing down my thoughts every day in a journal, possibly for want of anyone to tell them to, and on February 27 there is an entry that reads: 'The little white cat is still in the garden and answers to the name of Small.' After that I always had Small's birthday party on February 27 and I would tie a bow on her collar and ask a friend or two around to toast her good health. She became very well known by quite a lot of noted New Zealand writers and artists such as Peter Wells, Douglas Lloyd Jenkins, Robert Leek, Noel Virtue and his partner Michael Yeomans, Sheridan Keith, Mary McIntyre and so on. I do not know many people but Small was much noted by them all and would make a grand appearance looking very glitteringly white with pink paws and a secretive expression when they came to visit.

I got an idea at one stage, when writers were more often photographed for magazines and newspapers, that I would like to get Small's photograph in a magazine. It seemed the ultimate accolade for a starved albino animal that had once eaten beetles and spiders in a garden and had been observed by a thin, lonely, depressed woman from an upper window in a house by then sold. (Because Small and I moved about. She came with me to my little villa in Auckland in 1990 and we settled well there but got frightened off by burglaries. We took refuge for a while in an upstairs apartment where she viewed the passing traffic from a balcony on which I grew old roses. From there we went to a one-up, two-down Victorian cottage near the seafront in Devonport.) At that stage newspapers and magazines had a different way of reviewing New Zealand books: most of them would have a review and a photograph of you when you had a new book out. I always tried to get Small in a picture, but she was very timid about strangers and at the last moment would run off and hide. A photographer from, I think, *Cuisine* magazine nearly got her once when I was photographed sitting at the big dining table I had then and I had had to make a rice pudding. (There was a series of stories about writers and what they ate while writing books and I had said that towards the end of a novel I was so exhausted I just made a big rice pudding about every three days and ate a spoonful of it now and again. I remember that Witi Ihimaera said it was dreadful — digusting, I think he said — and we both laughed in that self-mocking way writers have. I said, 'But Witi, I do put sultanas in it.')

The photographer from *Cuisine* got me posed at the table with the big rice pudding in front of me and I was to have my picture taken dishing out a serving of it with a large, antique, silver spoon. At the crucial moment we both had our attention attracted somewhere, I cannot think why, and when we looked back at the pudding Small had jumped up on the table and was eating the pudding off the spoon.

That time we nearly got her picture but she sprang away just in time. I think that was the nearest I got to making her into what I called a cover girl.

At the time I found her in the old garden back in New

Plymouth she was about one year old, the vet said. She was not at all playful and was always quiet and watchful, perhaps because she had been very frightened. But one day, after she had been with me for several months, I heard an odd little noise which I could not identify at all. I went downstairs, round the three bends and down into the entrance hall, where I found Small playing with a dead leaf she had brought inside, and that was the first time I ever saw her play. I remember that I was very pleased because it meant she was feeling better and more secure and more carefree. I went to the supermarket and bought her some cat toys but she always preferred ping-pong balls to anything else. They were her favourite.

She got me into much better habits with eating and sleeping and that is why I wrote at the beginning of this story that she saved me. I think she did. I had to go out and buy food for her and thus I bought food for myself. Mostly we ate the same thing. The vet asked me once what she ate and I said, 'We eat the same.' I would buy a chicken and Small and I would share it. The same with steak or any other meat. I grew stronger and more interested in things. It was not so bad going home to the empty house if I went out because it was no longer empty. Small was there, always waiting. We became very tied to each other, I think, and were inseparable. She slept with me at night, curled up under my chin. This was hot in summer but warm in winter. Periodically during the night she would stir and place her cold nose on my cheek. I used her as a yardstick for a lot of things. People always rose or fell because of Small. By then I was slowly making a new life for myself because that is what you have to do. I remember inviting a local New Plymouth artist and his wife to visit once but never again because he made rude jokes about the immaculate Small and called her Smell. An admirer presented himself at the door one day and I thought, 'Oh well, one must be a pragmatist.' Small seemed to like him, which surprised me. She actually sat on his knee, so I regarded him more carefully. However, she had a habit of dribbling slightly when exceptionally pleased so when he noticed a tiny dab of something damp on the knee of his trousers he made a fearful fuss, to such an extent that I got him out the door smartly, never to return. Vanity and tantrums are not a good thing in a man, or anyone actually.

And I invented a legend about her, just secretly. I invented that George, wherever he was, had observed my despair and fright and had sent the little cat to me to be my friend. She had been bleached of colour by the terrible journey, and had also lost her tail. Thus I concocted a talismanic presence which heartened me. Sometimes, as I slept clutching Small, I dreamt of George, and the dreams were always the same. He was sitting quietly in a very plain wooden chair in a whitewashed room, reading a book. The book was on a little wooden table. And he turned the pages carefully, as if engrossed. I saw him only side-on in these dreams and I seemed to observe him from a corridor with an interior window. He looked calm, but as if he had been very ill. It was, perhaps, a sanitorium for those who have had fatal heart attacks. I seemed to be aware, in these dreams, that I was able only to observe and must not speak or make my presence felt. George was very shy and inward and it had worried me greatly when he died so suddenly that he would be deeply frightened and not know what to do. Again, like the legend of Small, this is ridiculous, but I used to awaken in the morning reassured, and clutching Small.

When I lived in the upstairs apartment, after all the burglaries, my elderly mother sometimes used to come to stay with me for a week or so. She would fly over from Sydney with a large, irregularly shaped suitcase from which she extracted various offerings.

'This is a nice warm jersey. It's a horrible colour, but it might come in handy in the winter.'

'Thank you, Mother.'

'Here are some biscuits. I opened the packet before I left but there are a few still left.'

'Thank you, Mother.'

Small became immediately devoted to her and deserted me completely for the duration of her visits. My mother, stationed by the doors leading out to the balcony, sat in a little French chair and either endlessly knitted or did her tapestry work. Small remained glued to her side. From time to time my mother put down an aged hand and grudgingly banged her on the head. Small seemed delighted. Every now and again my mother made one of two remarks and Small never took offence at either. The first was: 'I've always hated cats. Down on the farm we used to drown them.' Small gazed at her, entranced. The second was: 'Shame you haven't got that lovely curly hair like Geraldine.' This last one would be directed at me as I crouched, at bay at my desk, trying to finish *The Wedding at Bueno-Vista*. Geraldine was a distant cousin who had very curly hair.

One evening, during one of these visits, Small completely disappeared. After searching the apartment for her endlessly I put on a fit of hysterics in the hall. I said things like, 'All I care about is my cat. If my cat has disappeared I'm going to die,' and things of that sort. It went on for some time, during which I wept bitterly and very loudly. My mother continued to knit calmly and in the end said she was going to bed. When she flung up the lid of her suitcase to find her nightclothes we found that Small had put herself to bed in there, wrapped in my mother's voluminous and possibly grubby, pink, long-sleeved nightie. She seemed unmoved by the dramatic display that had been going on around her. (My mother was, sadly, never overly fond of bath water or washing in general. 'Just a little sponge is all it needs,' she would say gloomily when regarding the grubbiest garment. 'Washing ruins your skin and ruins your clothes. The trouble with you, apart from writing those terrible books, is that you've always used far too much soap.'

'Cleanliness is next to Godliness.' Sometimes I used to defend myself just a little.

'Rubbish. I'm not religious. And don't be cheeky.'

I could never win.)

When I was living in that apartment I found an explanation one day for some of Small's very mysterious disappearances. I was vacuuming the carpet in the sitting room and dragged the cleaner under the grand piano. While I was using the nozzle of the cleaner at point-blank range I noticed that, on the wide shelf under the piano, there was an accumulation of white fur. This meant that suddenly I had discovered where Small went when she was there one moment and gone the next. I often sat beside the piano crying bitterly because I could not find her and perhaps she was just a few inches away listening calmly, perhaps grinning a cat grin. Sometimes Small could be rather sardonic.

Another hiding place she had was on top of a very high Sheraton wardrobe I owned then. Sometimes I would search for her throughout the flat and then, at the end, would look up to find myself being regarded by a pair of cat eyes coolly gazing at me from behind an inlaid pediment, two feet from the ceiling.

Her sense of humour was often macabre. For instance, every night when I climbed into bed for eight years, she jumped out from under the bed and bit me on the ankle. I would obligingly scream. She awakened every morning at exactly 3.10 and had to be personally escorted to her saucer and given ten fresh cat biscuits, which she ate, and then we returned to bed. We then both went back to sleep. It was no use putting the biscuits in the saucer to await her arrival during the night because she would not tolerate it. They had to be fresh and I had to go with her.

We were very happy. She sat on my desk when I wrote and when I forgot the time and forgot to eat or go to bed Small tapped my hands with a paw to remind me. I cried into her fur when I was sad. She stayed with me devotedly if I was sick. I told her my secrets. We were inseparable. I loved her most dearly.

Small died when she was nine years old. She had lived with me for eight years. Suddenly one day she went down on her back legs and never got up again so she had to be put to sleep. I would have done anything to make her better again but nothing could be done. She was a feisty, courageous, unusual soul and being unable to walk around would have been terrible for her. The old injuries that had occurred before I found her had finally got her. I was bereft.

Grief is really a form of self-absorbed selfishness because one thinks of oneself and one's own loss. She could easily have died of her injuries when she received them, before I found her in my garden, so we had eight more years than that, more than a lifetime for some people. Some people die when they are born. Others live only a few months. Eight years of being happy is forever, really.

Some time went by. People tried to cheer me up. Peter Wells used to come over the harbour and take me for walks along the seafront. I grew used, again, to the feel of tears drying stiffly on my cheeks as I walked along in a brisk breeze off the sea. They feel like nail varnish. I used to have that feeling when I walked back home to the big house on the hill after George died. I walked most places then because I was frightened to drive the car. The impulse to drive into the side of a bridge or a tree, or anything, was irresistible.

One Saturday I returned to my one-up, two-down cottage to find a big black cat sitting on the front doorstep. Its fur was rather shabby as if it had come on a long journey. It had an aquiline face and a very gracious, benign manner, and followed me into the house, waving its tail. The cat seemed very much at home. I was rather startled but I found it something to eat and I imagined that it might have a bit of a rest and go on its way. I had never seen it before around the neighbourhood but it sat on the kitchen floor and regarded me in a sanguine manner and seemed comfortable. By the time night came it was still there and it came upstairs to bed. At exactly 3.10 it awakened and nudged me with its nose so I went downstairs, following the big black cat. It went and stood by the saucer. Wanting ten biscuits, I suppose — that is what I thought.

I gave it something to eat and we returned to bed.

When I took it to the vet to find out what it might need or want I was told it was a female aged about nine. No one advertised for her or claimed her or showed any interest in her at all, so I kept her, and I called her Gwendolyn. No one could be called Small ever again and for such a large, strong cat the name would have been absurd. Large did not seem to be a very pretty name for a cat, nor did Big. So she became my Gwendolyn.

And I invented another legend. I invented that she was my Small come back to me because I was so grief-stricken at her loss but she had come back to continue her life the opposite of what she had been. Instead of being a small, fragile, albino cat with no tail she had returned as a large, strong, black cat with a long tail. That is the whole story of my lovely Small and me.

poems

Janet Frame

The Cat of Habit

The cat of habit
knows the place by heart
or at least by space, scent, direction, bulk,
by shadow and light
moonlight starlight sunlight
and where to nest in each
with a three-focussed shut eye
on who or what's coming and going
on the earth and in the sky
and distantly, not present, the rays of inkling
shining within the furred skull.

The cat of habit curls her spine
in the most windless the most warm place
shivering a little with, 'It's mine',
an ear-twitch, tail-flip
of permanent ownership.

The cat of habit
has the place marked,
the joint cased.

Feed and sleep and feed
and half-heartedly catch
moths and mice and mostly watch
hourlong for the passing witch
for many, unseen, pass
through the rooms of the house and outside,
under the trees and in the grass.

A Golden Cat

As I walked to my office one day and stopped
by the flax bushes near the curve of the road
to look at the view of the city and Northeast Valley
and the amber poplars with the light shining through
    them,
and the autumn trees turning where turn still means
    decay,
the souring of the once freshly foaming season,
a golden cat came out of the bushes, wove
around my feet, said, Own me, Own me, I am golden.
Scorched flax, leaves, berries on fire, none
come so gracefully to you; it is I
who am weaving the golden season.

I hurried on thinking perhaps I dreamed it.

Diane Brown and Philip Temple

Catsitting

Pinned to the wall
a page of typed instructions:
Cornelius, the ginger half-Persian
(the one with the spoilt-child face
and all the evidence of gluttony)
sleeps in our bed at night
(that explains the hairs).
He'll sulk but might be consoled
by a saucer of warm milk
and cat talk, sweet kissy-kissy sounds
(or a warning with a raised boot)
I am serious, you two.

Lafayette the white one
(ears amputated after gangrene
accusing yellow eyes
as he claws the French doors)
is a diabetic requiring daily injections
of insulin; stroke his back
(grunge-white fur, a swinging belly)
and give him freshly grated cheese
(or pin him to the deck)
while you insert the needle.
If it's a good day
and you are feeling kind
you could give them fresh water.

He raises the syringe
'Wouldn't cyanide be kinder?
We could say he died of old age.'
'Don't count on it, cats
have nine lives,' she says
'and who knows what tales
he may live to tell.
It's entirely possible
we're already done for.'

Fiona Farrell

The Cat Climbs

There are few safe places.
The cat chooses the verandah roof.
Watch her climb the tree.
Watch her ebb about its roots.
Watch her flow against the trunk
and up paws lead body tail one
slow expansion watch her take
without rush each twig each
thorn marked hers with spit and
delicate attention. She notes the
flight of birds seeps through
leaves eases into her corner
quiet as spilt milk.

Jan Kemp

Night Poem

Port-Vila, New Hebrides '74

Beneath the liveries of day
lives a nightly cat
black beast
who prowls at stroke of three.
My sometime me
the late late show
when I miss
the innocent call to sleep.
She unlike the daytime self
wears sharper spectacles
no rose-tints. Her coat
sheens against the night
her stockings are seamed
a purple band winds round her hat
no sweet song lines her throat.
She strides the decks
some Lucifress to the night
she haunts stars fallen in the sea.
The moon lopes an ocean of cloud
ropes flack the mast
a bat comes sliding.
At four, peacocks cut the air
with scabbed voices.
Who is there here

but this sounding air
this dark this phosphorus
I splash from the sea?
She waits for that strike of furious light
a comet across her sky.

BERNARD BROWN

Mastersinger

Next time
on earth
I should most like
to be a large
unexpurgated
ginger tom,
with stripes;
tumescently whiskered,
I'd prowl on purpose
the hot nights yowling
like a catechist.

Daytimes I'd
lounge in the edge of the sun
being fussed, musing on
tonight's conquerable roof-
tops, and purr contentment
with the diminution,
by men's science,
of competitors.

short stories

MARGARET MAHY

The Cat Who Became a Poet

A cat once caught a mouse, as cats do.

'Don't eat me,' cried the mouse. 'I am a poet with a poem to write.'

'That doesn't make any difference to me,' replied the cat. 'It is a rule that cats must eat mice and that is all there is to it.'

'If only you'd listen to my poem you'd feel differently about it all,' said the mouse.

'O.K.,' yawned the cat, 'I don't mind hearing a poem, but I warn you, it won't make any difference.'

So the mouse danced and sang:

The great mouse Night with the starry tail
Slides over the hills and trees,
Eating the crumbs in the corners of Day
And nibbling the moon like cheese.

'Very good! That's very good!' the cat said. 'But a poem is only a poem, and cats still eat mice.'

And he ate the mouse, as cats do.

Then he washed his paws and his face and curled up in a bed of catnip, tucking in his nose and his tail and his paws. Then he had a little catnap.

Some time later he woke up in alarm.

What's wrong with me? he thought. I feel so strange.

He felt as if his head was full of coloured lights. Pictures came and went behind his eyes. Things that were different seemed alike. Things that were real changed and became dreams. Horrakapotchkin! thought the cat. I want to write a poem. He opened his mouth to meow, but a poem came out instead:

The great Sun-Cat comes up in the east.
Lo! The glory of his whiskers touches the hills.
Behold! The fire of his smiling
Burns on the oceans of the rolling world.

'Cat-curses!' said the cat to himself. 'I have turned into a poet, but I don't want to make poetry. I just want to be a cat, catching mice and sleeping in the catnip bed. I will have to ask the witch about this.'

The cat went to the witch's crooked house. The witch sat at the window with her head in her hands. Her dreams turned into black butterflies and flew out of the window.

She took the cat's temperature and gave him some magic medicine that tasted of dandelions.

'Now talk!' she commanded.

The cat opened his mouth to ask her if he was cured. Instead he found himself saying:

Lying in the catnip bed,
The flowering cherry over my head,
Am I really the cat that I seem?
Or only a cat in another cat's dream?

'I'm afraid it is too late,' said the witch. 'Your case is

hopeless. Poetry has got into your blood, and you're stuck with it for the rest of your life.'

'Horrakapotchkin!' cried the cat sadly, and he started off home.

But, five houses away from his own house, a black dog called Max chased him, as dogs do, and the cat had to run up a tree. He boxed with his paw at Max and went to hiss and spit at him, but instead he found himself saying:

Colonel Dog fires his cannon
And puts his white soldiers on parade.
He guards the house from cats, burglars,
And any threat of peacefulness.

The dog Max stopped and stared. 'What did you call me? Colonel Dog? I like that. But what do you mean — I fire my cannon?'

'That's your barking,' said the cat.

'And what do you mean — I put my white soldiers on parade?' asked the dog again.

'That's your teeth,' said the cat.

The dog wagged his tail. 'I like the way you put it,' he said again. 'How did you learn to talk like that?'

'Oh, it's poetry,' said the cat carelessly. 'I am a poet you see.'

'Well, I'll tell you what! I'll let you go without barking at you if I may come and hear that poem again sometime,' the dog Max said, still wagging his tail. 'Perhaps I could bring some other dogs to hear it too. Colonel Dog, eh? White Soldiers, eh? Very true.' And he let the cat go on home to his catnip bed.

If only he know, the cat thought. I wasn't meaning to praise him. Poetry is very tricky stuff and can be taken two ways.

The cat went on thinking: I became a poet through eating the mouse. Perhaps the mouse became a poet through eating seeds. Perhaps all this poetry stuff is just the world's way of talking about itself. And straightaway he felt another poem coming into his mind.

'Just time for a sleep first,' he muttered into his whiskers. 'One thing, I'll never eat another poet again. One is quite enough.' And he curled up in the catnip bed for a quick catnap, as cats do.

VINCENT O'SULLIVAN

Waiting for Rongo

Cards on the table then, as my former husband used to say, pretty nearly about anything. It's a straightforward-enough deck I have to deal from. I was married for over twenty years, I had one 'relationship', as they say, before marrying Thomas, and one after he passed on — rather than away. It doesn't sound so much, does it, one and one, making three like that over a lifetime? But I think I'm a fairly direct and sensuous woman — have been, at any rate — and have never thought a scorecard necessarily told one very much. I've liked the men I have been close to and there's nothing we did together that I wish we hadn't done. That's as close as I'll get to being explicit. I don't quite know how to put this even, but I've thought a few times when reading 'confessional writers' as they're called, that the 'confession' part can actually conceal, when of course it claims to tell all. I feel there's always a figure behind the curtain, you know what I mean?

My neighbour's name is Virginia Smith. I have no doubt whatever about the Smith, but the other I suspect may be something she plucked out for herself. I say this because a person knocked on the back door a few years ago and asked did I know Mrs Marty Smith's 'place of abode.' He gave the impression of having seen better times. ('Incorrigible,' Raymond laughed when I told him. He teases me for being a snob. As though anyone born near my end of Parnell Rise could be that, I reminded him. QED, he said.)

The man's heels in any case were worn down to the uppers. I told him I knew Mrs Virginia Smith but I had never heard of Marty. 'Close enough,' he said. Next thing I could see from the lounge window he was rat-tatting at her door and the moment it opened a cat took off from behind her leg and down the drive. 'Virginia' looked a sight but that did not seem to register with either of them. They were hugging as though they mattered to each other. 'You've got it in for that woman,' Raymond said. He said that first when we went to Fiji when the hotel rates were a song after the big dust-up the locals had together. A week in August, which is exactly when you need the sun and the rest of it. He said I should have asked her to keep an eye on the house. 'Neighbours like to be asked,' he said.

'There's neighbours and neighbours,' I reminded him. I said I'd rather pay a woman who was recommended to me at bowls. To take in the mail, move the curtains, switch on different lights on different days. You pay someone you don't know but can trust. There's no question then of asking favours.

'She's a pleasant woman,' he said.

So I told him, 'Raymond, don't take that cheery waving stuff for friendliness. It makes *her* feel good.' The way she waved if she ever caught us on the drive. Thank God the patio's on the other side.

'What would you call it, then?' He didn't often have that edge to his voice.

'I'd call it pushy, Raymond,' I said.

There must be half a dozen cats. Perhaps more. I don't mind

cats myself although only once, ten years back, I had one for the summer, until it disappeared. Stolen, I've always suspected. There were children across the road couldn't keep their eyes off her. 'She doesn't like being handled,' I told them, although she brought it on herself, running across to them the moment she saw them. So it's not as though I have anything against cats. But next door makes such a fool of herself with them. 'Here, darling. Here Rongo, pet.' That kind of thing, morning and evening. Stuff from the meat counter at the supermarket, too, nothing out of a tin.

'If that's what she wants to spend it on,' Raymond said.

'As if the same cardigan practically day in day out, as if brown Warehouse trousers summer and winter, isn't a case for something other than treating cats like royalty?'

Raymond enjoys talking with her. He says he likes 'her turn of phrase'. I tell him any Australian who half made it to a classroom door speaks better than she does. Even her surgery. She tells Raymond about her surgery. 'At my age, mind,' she had said, 'you don't go on doctors gawping at you, do you? I don't like it myself, to tell the truth. Saw myself in the mirror, the stomach like, next thing to a whipped suet pudding.' She laughs and spits into her handkerchief.

'She's vulgar but she's colourful,' Raymond defends her. I tell him you could say that about a baboon's backside.

This is starting to sound as if Raymond's right, as if I have it in for the woman. That isn't so. It is just her type, which is not mine. I said to the man who comes every fortnight to do the lawns, 'Doesn't it ever occur to her that a yard like hers lets the whole street down?' He's been coming for years. 'Your Grass is Ours' on the side of the van that carries his mowers.

He looks after them religiously. Each time he takes one down the ramp at the back of the van I say to him, so it's become a regular joke between us, 'Not another new mower, is it?' He's not a talkative man but he smiles at that. A smiling workman is a good workman, that's one thing I have learned over the years. But he disappointed me when I put that to him, about Virginia Smith, if that is her name, letting the street down. He did not look at me directly I must say, he made out he was tinkering with his machine. But what he said was 'Perhaps she doesn't think the rest of the street's worth worrying about.' It was hard to tell whether he was being offensive or not. Well I'll be looking in the ad columns under 'Lawns Cut' was what I didn't say to him. I think he knew he'd gone too far.

Strange how the unlikeliest things come back to you when you're half awake. Forty years ago Alex was halfway through his degree and lived in a run-down house ten minutes down from the Three Lamps, a house frankly that I told him would be the end between us and it was, although today you'd need a cool half-million even to think of it. Alex had a cat that was heavy as a child when it jumped on the bed. About as much character to it as a lump of coal. The first time it hurled itself up and landed like that it frightened me silly. Either shut the door when we're in bed Alex, I told him, or I'm calling it a day. 'He likes watching,' Alex said. He thought it amusing to twist things like that. Not that I was a prude or I wouldn't have been there in the first place. But I hadn't thought of that cat, obese and green-eyed and Lucifer, that was its name if you please, I hadn't thought of it for years and there was this thud and I could have sworn it was jumping on Alex's bed.

In fact it was Raymond putting out the bin, and the wheel had caught and the thing banged into the side of the house. But when I woke I could hear a cat and I was forty years back, and happy, that is the odd thing. It was as though the mood I must have had one morning back then still continued now, and everything in between had not taken place. And when it came in on me where I was, and how much later it was, I cried for five minutes in the bathroom. That kind of thing, it's completely out of character, I can tell you.

Later, Raymond said 'There's coffee on the patio, when you're ready.' I looked from the lounge window before I went out. Virginia Smith was standing in her yard with grass up to her knees. She was laughing as she tried to drag from her the cat that was climbing with its claws at her cardigan. I knew by now the creature was her favourite, its irregular head like a closed fist, an ear half missing, its body an ugly reddish colour, until a broad smear of pure white ran down its back legs. I thought, this is unreasonable, I know that, but how can one not detest that woman?

'You're all right are you?' Raymond asked me, when I joined him in the early September sun, and sat in the canvas chair and raised the coffee pot above my cup. His car keys were beside his own cup.

'I think I might just read today,' I said. 'I wouldn't mind a quiet day.' Mondays we usually drove around the bays, and had lunch looking across the harbour. My friend Linda, who is always hoping to improve me, has given me the life of a writer who ended up killing herself. I don't quite see how knowing the details of that will improve me. But I had kept the book for a fortnight as it was, and Linda will quiz me as she always does. I don't like the photograph of the woman on the cover, which is a bad start. She is leaner, mind you, and Caucasian as they come, but there is the same lank stringy hair, that same curious sense of certainty about herself, as Virginia Smith. Who would not, of course, know the first thing about the woman whose picture lies on my knee, looking straight through me.

'Those cats,' Raymond said. He is standing in the lounge at the window, watching the carry-on next door.

'Draw the curtains at least,' I tell him. 'She'll know you're looking.'

It is as though he has not heard me. He says instead, 'It's remarkable isn't it? The rapport, or whatever it is she has with them?'

'Give it a rest,' I tell him.

An hour later, by the end of the first chapter, I know I will not be going on with the book. Linda can say what she likes. It's the woman, an American, thinking she is so special, feeling miserable all the time. As if I want to spend another 200 pages on that, to get to the ending I already know.

There is a programme on television on Friday nights about people looking after animals. Pleasant young women in uniforms go round old people's houses checking their pets. Sometimes they are telephoned to pick up stray dogs, or take damaged birds to volunteers who nurse them back to again facing storms and skies. I said to Raymond, 'I know an address I wouldn't mind passing on.' It must have been one of the last evenings. He handed me a G and T with the lemon cut too thickly, but I told him, 'Thank you, my love.' Raymond was about to go to his daughter in Queensland for a fortnight. The last thing I wanted was to have an awkward moment before he left, so I said nothing when he said, as he leaned across and brushed his lips against my forehead, 'I'd look out another window for a while if I were you.'

So I tried. I spoke to Mrs Smith when we happened to be at our letterboxes at the same time. When she said she was dog-tired, this traipsing backwards and forwards to the hospital a couple of times a week, I offered her the opening I thought she would jump at. I said, 'Something they'll sort out for you pretty soon, I hope?' But she said oh you know what public hospitals are like, five minutes with a doctor and two hours of waiting. She looked at me so steadily I felt uncomfortable. I can say that now. At the time I thought it simply rude.

I saw her as usual after that, but avoided if I could more than having to nod to her. And of course I heard her calling her cats. Then a week after Raymond had left for Queensland there was a tap one evening, just after the News had started, on the back door.

'I'm sorry,' she said. 'I didn't realise the time.' She glanced past me to the television. I told her not to worry, it was not my favourite she interrupted. Irony was not in her repertoire. She stared at me for a long moment and then said, as though there were some effort in finding the words, 'I want you to do something for me.' She said the SPCA people had been that afternoon to collect her cats. I had been across to Linda's with the book I couldn't read, so I had missed the scene I could easily imagine. Virginia Smith did not say why she had asked the van to come round. 'Sergeant,' she said, and paused again. 'Sergeant wouldn't come down from the top of the wardrobe so they had to use a net. You know that big net they use?' It took ten minutes, she explained. She could hear him crying from the van. Then the favour she was asking me was that she didn't have the heart, not after this long, not with his eyesight going and his always being timid anyway, she couldn't bring herself to send Rongo off as well.

'Away?' I asked her. For a couple of weeks, that was all. Up north, she said. I could imagine her at her sister's, some modest house facing a beach. She could just walk across the road and there she would be, close enough to the sea to dip her feet in. Odd, isn't it, how that came into my mind? I suppose it was from seeing pictures of them on television, those scruffy little settlements that somehow struck you as idyllic.

Virginia Smith then picked up the plastic bag she had set down on the porch before I opened the door. It was heavy with cans of cat food. 'Not what he really likes,' she said, 'but it will do.' Once a day, she told me, on that bit of concrete near the under-house door. I needn't call him because he probably wouldn't come anyway, not so long as I was there. 'But I don't think he'd manage by himself, you see. Otherwise I wouldn't ask.' Then she said — as if I might have designs to keep the thing! — 'Just until I come back.' She became insistent. 'You will do that, won't you?' The fatigue drawing her face. It embarrassed me. I promised because I wanted her to go, when I knew I should have asked her more. About herself. About her sister. 'Rongo,' she said. 'You'll get to like him alright.'

It was a bad time, the next few weeks. Raymond rang to say his daughter was twisting his arm to stay on. When I repeated that, 'Stay on?', I expected him to say 'For a bit longer, love.' But what he said was, 'I don't know if there's much more mileage in it, do you? In us?' which brought it home with rather a thud. That he had known he would not come back. I then saw how little in fact there was of him still in the house. I realised how carefully, over weeks, he had moved so much back to the flat he had not properly lived in for over a year. I don't know why I hadn't noticed. The only jacket in the wardrobe was a herringbone, old fashioned and I expect now too small for him, that I had never seen him wear. The trousers on the hanger next to it were a pair he wore when he took the clippers to cut the hedge. A few razors, a few jars of unimportant pills.

Nor did my neighbour, of course, come back. She did not go north, and did not have a sister, but died in the local hospital, and only the names of two nieces, in a town two hundred miles away, were in the notice in the paper. A brother, who I suppose was the man with the worn heels. But Virginia was real. That was the name in the notice.

And here I am, on a late summer evening, standing in her back yard, the grass stalks rubbing against my legs. And my calling to him — 'Rongo'. Saying it quietly at first. And then louder, too loud, so that other neighbours may even have heard me. 'Rongo. Rongo, pet.' Wanting so much for him to come and take the food I have for him. Wanting his torn ugly head, his skinniness and rasping, wiry cry. Wanting him to watch at least from the corner of the house. Wanting him to know it is better here than anywhere else.

FRANK SARGESON

Sale Day

Victor poked his head in the kitchen door.

Anybody home? he said.

Elsie told him there wasn't. She was putting some chops on to fry, but the fire wasn't going any too good.

Victor pulled his shirt off, and went to have a wash in the scullery sink. There'd been a fire through the fern that he'd been cutting and he was pretty black.

It was sale day, and except for Victor the family had gone into town in the car. Before he'd gone the old man had sent Victor away up to the back of the farm to cut fern. He'd had to take his lunch which meant that Elsie had been left on her own all day. Usually there'd have been the cat for a bit of company. But it happened to be spring. And the cat was a tom.

Out in the scullery Victor made a lot of noise puffing and blowing and slopping water about, then he came back wet and soapy, and groped for his towel. He went over to the stove to dry himself, and Elsie got out of his way. She didn't look at Victor. She finished setting the table.

After a bit Victor flung the towel at a peg and it stuck on. Good shot, he said. He stood there slapping himself on the chest. He was a rather fine-looking young chap and he had plenty of muscle. Elsie turned round and looked at him.

You'll get your death of cold, she said.

Victor didn't say anything.

You ought to put your shirt on, Elsie said.

I will in a mo.

Your mother wouldn't have you standing about like that.

Mother doesn't appreciate a man's figure.

Elsie looked at him.

I like myself, I do, she said.

The chops began to sizzle a bit so Elsie went over to look at them and Victor moved aside. Then the cat walked in. It looked pretty thin on it. It stood just inside the door and made a meow at Victor, but you couldn't hear anything.

Hello cat, Victor said.

Silly, Elsie said, call him by his proper name.

Victor stamped his foot at the cat and it crouched but it didn't run.

He stinks, he said. He's randy.

Puss, Puss, Elsie said.

The stinking brute. Don't encourage him.

Pussy cat, Elsie said.

I don't like randy tom cats.

Come on pussy cat, Elsie persisted, where've you been all day?

You'd hate him if he was a she.

Go on, Elsie said, I'm fond of animals.

Elsie turned over the chops with a fork. They weren't sizzling any too good, so she put the pan over the open fire.

I don't particularly like myself, Victor said. Any more than I like that cat.

I'll believe you if you put your shirt on.

I thought you were fond of animals.

Well, I am.

Only randy tom cats.

Elsie didn't say anything.

The cat was pruning its whiskers against the leg of the table. Its tail stuck up straight. Elsie went on talking to it and the cat said meow, but you couldn't hear anything. It was so thin it looked silly.

I hate the sight of it, Victor said. It's randy.

If I hadn't had jobs in hotels I wouldn't know what randy is.

It's just a word, Victor said. A bloody good one.

He left off slapping himself and stroked his muscles instead. The chops were sizzling properly now, and Elsie gave them another turn over.

D'you know, Elsie, Victor said, I nearly came home for lunch.

Elsie didn't say anything.

Yes, I did, Victor went on.

Elsie looked at the clock.

It's time they were home, she said.

High time, Victor said.

The cat came and rubbed itself against Elsie's legs, and she bent over to stroke it.

Don't touch him, Victor said. The randy brute stinks.

It's only nature, Elsie said.

You're nature too, Elsie. So am I.

Well, what about it?

That's what I say. What about it?

Pussy cat, Elsie said.

Nature's bloody awful, Victor went on.

Oh, go on. Put your shirt on.

In a mo. I've got a sensitive nature, Elsie.

Didn't I say you liked yourself?

You're wrong Elsie. And I don't like you kidding to randy tom cats.

Elsie looked at him.

I believe you're cracked, she said, and she picked the cat up and nursed it.

Living all your life on a farm you see too damn much of nature, Victor said. It's no good if you've got a sensitive nature yourself.

You want to take life as it comes.

I bet that's what you did. You're engaged, aren't you Elsie? Give us a proper look at the ring.

No I won't. You can see it good enough.

Well, tell us about the lucky bloke.

That's my business.

O.K. Have it your own way.

They stood there, and Victor went on stroking his muscles. Elsie stroked the cat and it started to purr.

I jolly near did come home for lunch, Victor said.

I wouldn't have cared, Elsie said.

That's what you say.

Well, you heard me.

Say I had come home for lunch, Victor went on. The cat wasn't home then.

Elsie poked at the chops with her fork. They were doing now a bit too fast.

I'll hold the cat, Victor said, and he took it. He held it up by the legs with both hands and the cat hung down in a curve, but it didn't leave off purring.

Filthy brute, Victor said.

They're done, Elsie said, poking at the chops. I wish they were home.

She lifted the pan a bit and you could see that the fire was hot underneath.

You want to lift the pan right up, Victor said. They're burning.

Well, Elsie lifted the pan and Victor dumped the cat in the fire. Elsie just stood there, and Victor grabbed the pan and jammed it down on top of the cat.

Then, not far away, you could hear the car, and Victor went over to put his shirt on.

Look here, Elsie, he said, it's a fortnight to next sale day. If I was in your shoes I'd look round for another job.

SARAH QUIGLEY

Q: So Where Do All the Cicadas Go?

A: They are dismembered on her floor.

A long time afterwards, this was what she remembered. Walking barefoot on cicada legs. Round shiny thighs like the glazed drumsticks of chickens, thin hairy feet. Merlin brought in many, every day. And left them dismembered for her to walk on.

The heat became fused in her mind with the sound of cicada voices. When she opened the door every morning, the heat and the voices would flood into the empty night apartment. When she left the house she felt as if she was pushing against a swelling balloon of hot insistent breath.

Every tree chattered. Every tree was a potential graveyard whose inhabitants would end up on her floor.

*

'I despise the way cats eat.'

That was Sonya's voice from that summer. Merlin ate tuna from a floral china bowl, tossing the delicate flakes from one side of his mouth to the other. The disc on his collar sang against the rim of the china bowl and Sonya said,

'I despise the way cats eat.'

*

It was a year and six months since they had seen each other but then and now it was summer. Today the tarmac at the airport would not stay still and passengers walked on shimmering legs from the planes. Greer was early and watched from the observation deck. She hadn't practised any opening lines because she didn't think she'd need any.

The moment is strange, when you see someone emerging from customs but can't do anything because they're still too far away. Do you smile and keep smiling until the layers of people between you have peeled away? Sonya, for instance, gave one wave and then kept her eyes down for the length of the yellow barrier, so they had to recognise each other for a second time.

But their excitement was real and uncontained. Their desire to recapture themselves ran strongly beneath the surface like an undertow.

'You drive like an Italian,' complimented Sonya.

'Just making you feel at home,' said Greer.

'And you, you feel at home here?' said Sonya. Her arms were olive though she'd come from a Florentine winter. Her left arm rested on the window and the sun lit the fine dark hair which lay smoothly in one direction.

'I guess so,' said Greer. She looked around at the green paddocks and air hangars, and the motels. She no longer thought about it so she supposed she must.

*

The first drink they shared was chamomile tea, the colour of the afternoon. Sonya stepped down off her platform shoes.

'Tell me where you've been since Italy,' she said. Her hair

hung straight over one shoulder and a faint dark sheen was on her upper lip.

'Nowhere really,' said Greer.

'Holidays?' asked Sonya rhetorically.

'No,' said Greer. The need for an explanation played in the air above her cup. She waved it away. 'I've been saving for a place.'

'This apartment isn't yours?' asked Sonya. She sounded surprised and her hand lifted off the sofa as if it no longer wanted to rest on rented property. But it was reaching for her tea.

*

This is the strange truth. Greer watches her friends go on holidays and is no longer sure if she is envious. When she needs a change of scene, she visits her living room.

This is what Greer does. When she knows the light from her bedside lamp so well that she can't breathe anymore, she takes her duvet and walks like an Indian to the living room. She lies down on the sofa. And this is enough.

When she wakes, lying narrow and straight on an unfamiliar surface, she is renovated. Waking is earlier than in her bedroom because in another room she can break routines. She leaves the blinds open so that at 5 a.m. the silver light can creep in and under her eyelids. The window is open, or not — it doesn't matter. She has been away.

Most of the time, she knows that all you need is an alternative. Then you have freedom.

*

Sonya looks slightly different. It may be the surroundings: the change from marble domes to flimsy office-blocks. Here, now, she is more than statuesque. Her head lowers the ceiling of Greer's flat by a couple of feet. But —

'You've changed,' she says authoritatively to Greer.

She stands at the bedroom door which now looks child-sized. Her glossy skirt stretches across her hips like a fitted sheet slightly too small for the bed. Greer looks at the lines in the fabric, five taut lines like a stave. She wants to pencil in notes, make music from Sonya's skirt.

'Changed how?' Greer says.

'You've put on weight,' says Sonya. 'No, maybe you've lost it.'

'Huh,' says Greer. She feels like saying, make up your mind. The heat is growing and, unusually, is making her irritable.

*

Her flat looks over a square where skateboarders jump. She envies the moment when they are balanced in nothing: there is no equivalent in everyday life. Their wheels spin free of concrete and their sunglasses absorb their narrow faces. This is true privacy.

Skateboards roar through her sleep: planes across a clouded vault. When she wakes up, she can smell smoke. It is Sonya, having a cigarette in the kitchen.

'You don't mind, do you?' she says rhetorically.

'Whatever,' says Greer. She stumbles for the toaster.

'You do,' says Sonya. (So she still recognises Greer.) 'I'll take you out for breakfast then.'

'It's OK,' says Greer. 'You should save your money.'

'Why?' says Sonya, looking amused. 'What for?'

'I don't know,' thinks Greer. 'The future.'

'This is my future, now,' shrugs Sonya. 'This is what I've saved for.'

*

Greer took two weeks off work to show Sonya around. She planned each day lying in her bed the night before. She didn't have a car so they had to walk.

'You walk so fast,' complained Sonya. She preferred to wander, while Greer was used to striding.

'Is it much further?' Sonya said. Her steps slowed every time they passed a bag shop.

'The view's worth it,' said Greer.

They entered the Domain. The cicadas roared above them. They climbed brown hillsides which crackled under their feet. The museum had never seemed so far away and when they got there the harbour looked small and faded.

Greer was sweating. Sonya didn't say anything about the view. She sat on the steps and took out her cigarettes.

'Is there a café around here?' she asked.

'There's a tea shop inside,' offered Greer.

'It's like England here, no?' said Sonya. Her rising inflection sounded theatrical, almost absurd. 'Everyone drinks tea.'

'No we don't,' said Greer. 'We're actually a nation of coffee drinkers.'

The clouds swept across the harbour with quite astonishing beauty but it was too hot, and too late anyway because both their minds had gone somewhere else.

*

A thunderstorm with the violence and passion of opera. Even though it was the middle of the afternoon, their faces shone white in the darkness. The rain spent itself in dark coins on their coats and on the surface of the Arno.

It seemed important not to run for cover like everyone else. They stood and watched the storm sweep low like witches over the orange roofs. Lightning grabbed the sky and ripped it in half, and in half again.

Uno due they counted to see how close the thunder was, and held each other's arm. *Uno due tre* and the long train of thunder rushed towards them.

When the low sky was pulled away like a rug, revealing clear blue space, they walked through deserted streets. By the time they got up to Piazza Michelangelo, where they were meeting friends, the ground was steaming.

'*Bella!*' men called out to them. '*Bellissima!*'

Greer's dress was not designed for thunderstorms and had gone semi-transparent. Sonya laughed and draped her arm round Greer's shoulders and over her breasts.

Greer bought an umbrella from a vendor whose awning drooped with water.

'Ees strange, no?' he said.

'What?' she said.

'Most people buy umbrellas before the rain start,' he said.

Greer and Sonja lay on their backs on the drying parapet and laughed. The wind dried Greer's dress to a stiff dishcloth feel. It rustled against her thighs as she laughed.

The feeling of laughing lying down is like no other. Your stomach rises to meet the sky and your laugh is pushed into an upward arc like water from a drinking fountain. Your mouth trickles down each side of your face. From the side it probably looks as if you are crying.

*

The second night was a dinner for Sonya. Miles arrived first. He looked slightly odd and his hair, usually unkempt, was still that way but looked somehow conscious.

'Are you OK Miles?' whispered Greer. They had gone into the kitchen to open wine but since there were no walls between Greer's kitchen and living room, she had to whisper.

'Yeah,' said Miles, looking surprised. 'Why?'

The wine he had brought was a South African white. 'Sonya?' he said.

'Oh sure,' answered Sonya. 'It's OK to drink South African wine now, isn't it?'

This could have been a joke or it could have been a serious comment. Greer groped her way through the possibilities. But Miles seemed to know what to do and he poured Sonya a glass.

'Politically it's OK,' he answered. 'But gastronomically, of course, Italy rules.'

Sonya looked pleased, Phil and Jenny started talking about the Springboks, and Greer traced the conversation with one finger. It was as if she was reading a book in a second language. Every time she went to the kitchen area it was harder to find her place when she got back.

They spread a map of Europe out on the floor and Greer and Sonya retraced their travels for the others before they ate. The fettucine stuck together like long hair in need of a wash and the sauce was very salty. Greer sucked her lip and talked of the Red, and the Dead, seas.

Even after the pasta the evening seemed taut. Jenny's jokes bounced tentatively on its surface and rolled unnoticed into corners. Greer became preoccupied with the lighting, which seemed both harsh and flat. She turned off lights, switched others on, but never struck quite the right combination.

*

That night she could hear a mosquito whining. She switched on her lamp and saw it above her bed, cruising like a fighter pilot, legs hanging menacingly.

'You're in for it you bastard,' said Greer. She leapt and twisted.

'What're you doing?' called Sonya from the sofa.

'Just a mozzie,' Greer called breathlessly.

'I don't know what you're talking about,' came Sonya's voice, 'but could you stop thumping?'

Greer went to the bathroom with a black carcass on her hands. In the white light she looked down on a smear of dark red. She had been asleep in her own house and suddenly she had the blood of someone else on her fingers.

She grabbed the soap and washed her hands until they squeaked.

*

They went to get Sonya's photos developed. Sonya stuck a feather in her hair like a catwalk model. She attracted looks as they walked.

They bought cappuccinos at a coffee stall and sat on a bench at the side of the footpath. Two builders walked past to order their morning tea.

'There goes Hiawatha,' said one of the guys. They both sniggered. Sonya didn't hear, or perhaps she didn't understand. She smiled to herself.

'Shall we go?' she said to Greer, still smiling.

Later Greer picked up the feather which was lying on the coffee table. She looked at the quill end of it, scratched it against her face. It had the brittle irrelevance of a toenail. Inside, in its transparent tube, it was full of dead skin cells.

*

Greer misses her living room. It wakes her up in the night — the knowledge that she can't go there until daylight hours. One night she even gets up and walks to the door, which is slightly open. She can hear Sonya breathing, a loud, even sway. She can't see the lights of the city because the blind is pulled down.

Greer leans there with her head against the wall until she is almost asleep. She reels and wakes and goes back to bed, but there is a deep, dragging ache inside her like a period pain. She tries to diagnose it. Is she homesick for her living room?

*

Merlin woke Sonya up every morning by jumping in the window onto her face. For the first three mornings Sonya didn't say anything and after that she shut the window.

'But he has to come in and out when he wants!' said Greer.

'Why?' said Sonya calmly.

The heat got fiercer. The dry wind blew at night, but still Sonya slept with the window shut. When she walked to the bathroom in the morning the small coils round her hairline were plastered to her skin and sweat sat on her upper lip.

'I wish the heat would go away,' Greer complained.

She hovered over the table like a canopy threatening to fall.

'It doesn't bother me,' said Sonya. She sat back on her chair and lit a cigarette.

'Sorry,' she said, and stubbed it out in the lid of the jam. 'It doesn't bother me,' she said. 'In Florence it gets far hotter than this.'

Greer knew this. Greer had been to Florence, had lived and worked in Florence. Sonya knew that Greer knew, and Greer knew Sonya knew. There was so much knowledge in the kitchen that the air crackled and Merlin backed out of the room.

*

Greer had had a job delivering pizzas. She didn't have an international driver's licence but riding a moped in Italy was like walking anywhere else. Sometimes she would career round to Sonya's and take her for a ride.

One night she was parking in the alley when a guy flashed at her. She just stood there, staring at him as he pulled down his shorts and exposed himself. When she went into the lobby of Sonya's building, she pressed the button of the lift and as she did so, she lost her personality. It was as sudden as that. One minute she had been Greer in the alleyway, with a past and a face. The next an elderly man had shown his genitalia to her and she had become anybody. Any body, related to in a completely anonymous way.

She could have shot him dead for doing this to her. She didn't recover herself until she reached Sonya's door and heard Sonya call her by her name.

*

After a week they had been to many movies and eaten many dinners. Sonya wanted something different.

Greer took her to a bar where there were many thin and languid people. All the windows on the street side were open but no air moved through. Groups stood still and breathed carbon monoxide and smoke.

'We are surrounded by stultification,' said Greer but her voice was lower than the music. She fell silent.

Sonya started talking to the barman out of self-defence. Greer left her there and walked thirty minutes home, through pockets of warm air that the day had left behind.

She woke much later to hear grunting and cries from the living room. She lay stiff and straight in her bed but a hot flush washed over her like water. The sofa creaked urgently through the wall and Sonya's moans rose above the cicadas. Greer wanted to get up and close the door but instead she concentrated on the drop of sweat outlining her eye socket.

When she heard the toilet flush and the front door open and close, she turned at last in her bed. She tried to find sleep but it had left her long ago. Her single sheet was clammy and the blind moved like a heavy sightless moth at the window.

*

She woke to hear Sonya shouting.

'*Via*!' she heard. '*Via*!'

The living room was garish with mid-morning sun. Merlin was savaging a cicada in Sonya's Italian shoe. The giant head stared from the floor but the body was still buzzing under Merlin's jaws. Sonya was holding her wrist.

'He's a wild animal!' she said.

'Give it up, Merlin,' Greer said. She bent down to empty the shoe. A growl muttered deep in Merlin's chest like thunder. He slashed at Greer and a thin white line appeared down one side of her finger. Anger welled with the blood.

'Little shit!' she said, grabbing for Merlin.

Merlin ran to the bedroom and skidded under the bed, his ears flattened. Greer dragged him out and shook him until his eyes changed colour. His head was thrown back and she noticed a gauze wing caught in his teeth.

Sonya left for the airport in a taxi with a plaster on her wrist. She and Greer hugged on the roadside.

'See you later,' they said. '*Ciao.*'

See you later. It's a safe phrase, an umbrella term which turns the rain of definition. Mastered early by New Zealanders, it is brought out even on occasions when it is plainly a final meeting.

Ciao, it has slipped easily into the international dictionary of greetings and partings. Unlike the French *adieu* and *au revoir*, ciao requires no forethought or decision-making. It enables you to part without commitment.

So with these short words, distance grows between the two figures. One sitting in a cab, one standing on the footpath, both waving.

Inside a cat waits to forget, or forgive.

Outside, unseen armies of cicadas chant out another summer on a dying fall.

PETER WELLS

My Dear Gabrielle

'I only eat ice cream and chocolate.'

Molly Cummins stared down at the child. 'Well,' said Molly, a little too tartly — her eyes searching for one iota of family resemblance in the changeling's face, 'you won't find any round here.'

But the child was already ahead of her.

'What about that ice-chest there?' And the child indicated with an almost weary nod of her head the freezer which stood, somewhat respendently, on the linoleum squares. 'You gotta have ice cream in there.'

Molly turned her face away. She was grinning like a skull. Penny, her own daughter, had been notoriously picky about food. Molly's early motherhood was a crucifixion ranged round what Penny would, and wouldn't eat. Naturally there were medical symptoms. Penny had been diagnosed as hyperglycaemic. It only seemed just that Penny had had, in turn, a child who ate for breakfast, as she so brazenly said, 'ice cream and chocolate'.

The fact that these luxurious items were enumerated in an American accent only sealed the deal for Molly. It was game, set and match as far as she was concerned. She did not comprehend Penny's child just as she did not understand her own daughter. Why, for example, did her only child have to go and live almost as far away from her and Stan as it was possible to get? Penny had gone, on a scholarship, to a university in North Carolina, and then, marrying an obscure American — 'a nice enough lad all things considered' as Stan said laconically — they had set up house — obstinately — on that far side of the world.

Molly and Stan had visited them twice, carefully parsing out the time spent with their daughter and her new family so neither party, as it were, became exhausted with examining the truths of either ménage. Besides Molly knew, as far as Penny was concerned, the game was all up. Penny had grown up in a family atmosphere of almost constant sniping. Molly and Stan had married during the War: Stan had gone overseas. On his return Molly and Stan were virtual strangers, each travelling as far away from the other in the adventures each had had in the War: both had suffered and lost.

Stan had experienced the lunacy and super-normality involved in hunting down and killing other humans. Molly had fallen in love with a woman, in the Land Army. The affair was passionate but at war's end, Molly's woman friend had got married. Molly and Stan came back together as battle-hardened warriors to some extent. Yet instead of going their separate ways, they had decided — more out of exhaustion than anything — to stay together. Penny was the result.

Penny who could not wait to leave home. Penny who left home the moment she turned sixteen. She had gone flatting and effectively drifted out of Molly and Stan's life. Or rather, the daughter for Sunday dinner once a fortnight was some kind of hostage returned to the fold, changed by her experiences.

One weekend Penny came home announcing she believed in abortion on demand and 'free sex'. Another weekend she had false eyelashes. Another time she was curiously without make-up, silent, almost chastened. Molly had found her weeping in her old bedroom. But when she tried, hesitatingly, to comfort her daughter Penny had turned on her. She had said some of the cruellest things anyone had ever said to Molly. How she had tried to stifle Penny. How she was jealous of the freedom Penny had. How she wanted Penny to have the kind of miserable non-existence Molly had. The words 'female eunuch' were used.

Molly had gone into her bedroom and lain on the vast ice cube of a double bed, immobile with grief. Stan had, for once in his life, taken Molly's side. 'Go in and apologise to your mother,' Molly heard, keenly listening even as she lay there, 'mortally wounded' as she put it. Penny had apologised through pursed lips. Following that she did not return for over six months. By this time Molly sensed, knew in every fibre of her being, that Penny was free: she had a lover, or lovers, was on the pill. Brazenly Penny surveyed the mute silences of her parents' lives. She judged them failures. She could hardly wait for the scholarship which would deliver her to freedom.

So she had disappeared. The two visits they had had in the following decades only underlined how deeply different their worlds were. Gabrielle, the infant, for a while, had been a unifying focus. Molly proudly placed a photo of the babe inside her purse so she could produce it, flourishing it as some kind of identity card which implied her place in the human race. But gradually this photo came to have a greater reality than the child itself who, anyway, was growing and had been growing ever since that moment when the camera button had clicked. Stan and she returned to their mutual, prickly silences. Molly escaped to her bowls club as much as possible while Stan, retired, did the lawns with an almost obsessive attention to the straightness of lines. Each attended to their wounds in silence. They no longer argued so intensely. They were united by one thing — and it was not, rather unfortunately, that infant growing up day by day far away from them in America. It was a cat.

Stan and Molly had a tom, a moggy as Molly liked to say. He was a cat who was generously black all over, slow moving as he got older. He was a good ratter. At moments of capture and torture, he seemed to grow into himself, gaining both bulk and stature. It was as if he were magnified at these moments: more essentially the hunter, the male, than he ever was at those longer, more lethargic moments when he lolled, at the end of the drive, under the grapevine, gazing through half-opened lids at the little white-eyes who, so dangerously yet flirtatiously, darted from leaf to leaf overhead.

Imagination was neither Stan nor Molly's forte — they called the cat almost by mutual consent (and hence one of the few things they ever agreed on) *Blacky*. Blacky was the cement in their lives, he glued them together. Their hands only ever touched, and then glancingly, when both reached down to the magnetic warmth of the beast's back. Blacky seemed to comprehend his role. He was impartial in his comfort offerings. To Stan he offered rubs around the leg, companionship in Stan's Sisyphean occupation of mowing the lawn wherein Blacky stood a certain way off, on a high point, as if supervising. This offered Stan many opportunities for conversation. 'Warm day, isn't it Blacky?'

At first Stan, a meagre spender of words, had felt self-conscious about *speaking to a cat*. Would people think him barmy? But in the end, when the choice was between an endless void of silence — Molly and he exchanging at best four or five sentences a day — and the soft roundelays of words he passed on to the wise cat: *there was no choice. People could think him mad. He would die one day soon. Stan could wait no longer. He would prefer people to think he was insane than spend his life immersed in the horrid cauldron of endless, eviscerating silence.* Many sad and thoughtful conversations passed between the old man and the wise cat. Stan caressed him when he had a chance, unobserved.

Blacky offered other things to Molly. He sat on her knee while she watched television and knitted. He warmed her cold thighs. She fed him. Molly too occasionally allowed herself to express her secret hurts. Her sense of isolation, the way Penny did not ever write. Her excitment when Penny, now divorced, announced she was coming home for a Christmas visit. Bringing the changeling with her. The one who only ate, as she proclaimed, 'ice cream and chocolate' for breakfast.

Of all the horrid, spoilt . . .

Molly shocked herself with her almost bilious dislike of the child. She had been prepared for some kind of girly cuteness. Thinking of her eight-year-old granddaughter, she had lingered at the mall before almost pornographic excesses of baby-doll girls' clothes. There were crinkly ginghams, little puff sleeves with silk ribbons threaded through, pleated Scots kilts and party dresses of filmy organza. She had, daringly, bought a pink gingham dress, splurging out of the tiny amount of housekeeping she managed to squirrel away. (Stan each week, on a Sunday morning, sat down and investigated her accounts. No audit by the Inland Revenue could match his searching eye.)

Molly had undergone paroxysms of silent joy while the items were being wrapped. She saw, in her mind's eye, the little girl unwrapping the gifts: she could almost feel her phantom warmth as she hurtled into Molly's outstretched arms. She would be Penny, except made warmer, less hurtful, less angular.

Except, of course, Gabrielle was like a version of Penny made more intense. Everything Molly had found difficult to accept in her daughter — her truculence, her obstinacy — her untidiness, her strange dietary habits — the necessity to speak her mind: everything seemed to have arrived at the perfect vortex of this unlikeable, assertive child.

All three of them were staring at the freezer.

It was big enough to hold a body.

'Well —?' said Molly, aware that Penny was surveying her. She did not want to replicate her old mistakes with Penny. Mutely she flicked a glance at her daughter. But Penny had been knocked off her perch by the divorce. She was no longer quite the old rebellious warrior of gung-ho. She had a new kind of tentativeness, almost a nervousness, a sort of hesitation which Molly recognised, as if staring within the duchesse mirror of an earlier existence.

'Now Gabe, you promised to eat everything while you're staying with relatives . . .'

Penny had an ameliorative tone. Molly winced, silently,

at her daughter's North American accent. In it she read loss, accusation, distance.

The child gazed, assessingly, at her mother and the stranger who was technically her grandmother. 'Mom,' the prodigy said. 'I feel like some exercise. Why don't you and I take ourselves off to chew off some fat?'

From the front-room window, Molly watched the two march away. She had the sense her daughter was being driven along like some kind of sacrificial slave in awkward-looking athletic shoes. The child was darting ahead, uncomfortably energised for eight o'clock in the morning.

It was that awkward hiatus between Christmas and New Year. Each year this low tide of time always delivered Molly and Stan back to each other with an almost malicious brio. Everyone they knew was involved, as people said, '*with family*'. Even those to whom the term meant hell on wheels always managed to get a certain self-congratulatory medal in the tone.

This year Molly had the comfort of saying flutingly over the phone, 'we're busy *with family*'. Yet the celebrations, as such, had almost come to grief over the grandchild's dietary imperium. Gravy, almond icing, vegetables, meat — in fact food in any unprocessed state — was received by the child as an attempt to covertly poison. Stan had withheld his usual coruscating barbs for an overlong period. Then he had unleashed: *ungrateful, wasteful* were a few of the terms he used. Penny knew he was talking about her. Stan took himself off, and sulked in the garden with his companion Blacky.

Molly had taken away plates of uneaten food. With tears stinging her lashes, she had scraped the plates straight into the bin. She normally placed, under the seal of plastic, little mouse-portions of leftovers into the deep-freeze. She no longer cared. She was surprised by the savagery of her desolation. So this was a family Christmas? So this was the ugly little secret everyone held so tightly to their breasts? Strangers came together and wounded each other in ways only intimates knew.

The house was silent now. It was a relief. Perhaps Penny had taken the ungrateful child away somewhere for an ice cream. Molly replayed again in her mind the child opening, then discarding her presents. 'Gabrielle doesn't wear dresses,' Penny had said in an apologetic, newly humbled tone. Penny had looked into the bruises in her mother's eyes. For a moment mother and daughter hesitated on some kind of confidence. Instead Molly stooped down and, again in a first, crinkled up all the Christmas wrapping, announcing to the walls, 'We might as well get rid of everything.' When she regained her self-possession, she announced, as if serenely to the silent couple, 'I can take it all back. Get a refund. That's the nice thing about Christmas, isn't it? You can take things back.'

The child had gazed across the chasm at her grandmother. Like some kind of animal she seemed to diagnose she had given, unwittingly, the gift of pain. She had wounded the old woman with her careful table settings, unimaginative floral arrangements of holly and pine cones brought out year by year, like some kind of shrieving.

'Look . . . Grandmom?'

Gabrielle hesitated for only a moment, as if to choose the correct term for this slightly forbidding stranger. She held up, in her hands, two *problems*, as Molly instantly foresaw them. Two smoke-grey kittens. Probably less than a month old, they had the almost blind-sighted look of the newly minted.

'Can I keep them? Oh, can I?'

Gabrielle had changed into a little supine human, finally finding something she could love. She fumbled with the kittens, patting them, holding them out before her. Small claws tried, ineffectively, to maul.

Both kittens, Molly saw, had collars, a little bell.

'They belong to someone. Where did you find them?' Stan had come up from the garden, standing at the back door in his garden boots.

'Where are they from?' he asked.

'We were walking back through the park. Gabrielle heard them. I didn't. They were crying. Stuck up a tree.'

'We can keep them, can't we Grandmom?'

Almost unconsciously, Molly warmed to the way the child had so suddenly and easily slotted the term into her mouth. The child gazed up at her, her plain, freckled face almost poignant with longing.

'Can I?'

You'll be going home soon, she didn't say. You can't take them on the plane. For one moment everything went into a delay. 'We'll get a carton. Stan? And pop them in. Someone's gone away, no doubt, leaving them with a neighbour to feed. They must have wandered away.'

Stan's eyes for a moment — and this was so unusual as to make her feel as if she were suddenly naked — touched her own. Molly was almost overwhelmed by a memory: she was in a darkened room, undressing, and Stan was there. This was in the very first cadenza of their marriage. She found herself blushing, or at least feeling a warmth driving down from her forehead. The kitten's helpless mewling brought her back.

'We must give them some food. Just a little. They look like they're starving.'

The kittens ate with the rare concentration of the famished.

'But not too much.'

Gabrielle, in her boyish shorts and t-shirt, looked up with new appreciation at her grandmother.

'Why not? Aren't they hungry still?'

'They'll be sick. Their stomachs need to get used to the idea of food.'

Gabrielle would not move away from the beer carton.

'Look, they're sleeping now.'

The breathless bulletins were delivered to her gran. Penny went down into the garden. Stan was standing there, his foot resting on Blacky's stomach. The old cat was lying on his back, exposing his stomach to the old man. But such was the trust between these two that neither moved to advance the scenario, and so they stayed, still as statues, connected, unmoving. Penny stopped where she was, and watched. She had the curious feeling of time moving away from her, so she suddenly felt she was back being the teenager who had never left. It was one of those endless Sundays, somewhere between being enjoyable for the fact nothing happened and full of apprehension verging on horror that nothing ever would. She was captive and mute.

'Dad?' she called out after a moment.

They had once been friends. Until Penny had — well,

developed breasts. Then he had not liked what she had become. She sensed his dislike which hardened, in time, into disapproval and the hard-nugget words like *tart, protester, stirrer.*

'How old is Blacky now?'

She held in her memory a few stray pages, like photos placed almost absent-mindedly in a book. These were images of Blacky as a younger cat. Because she was growing as the cat was growing they had almost passed each other by, seemingly going in opposite directions. Now she realised they had been moving alongside each other all the time. Her father would die in the foreseeable future. The cat too would possibly die within the same period. As if glimpsing the vast veldt of her mother's aloneness when this occurred, she knelt down by the cat.

'He must be, oh, sixteen at least.' The old man paused to consider. 'We got him when you were . . . eight?'

Blacky's peeled-grape eyes moved to her. He looked up at her not exactly without recognition but with something more familiar: a disdainful suspension of trust: something mocking and knowing. *I shall be here when you are gone. I am the one this old man touches and communes with. You are an interloper.* Or was this, Penny judged, marijuana paranoia. She had managed to get a doobie from an old mate in Ponsonby and had had a toke while Gabrielle explored in the park.

The cat arched back to its fullest extent. His black fur was speckled with straws of white, as if individual hairs had been caught in paint.

'He's getting old,' Penny said, instantly regretting her words.

'He's a good cat,' Stan said, in answer.

The cat flopped on its side, then went into a frenzy of biting and scratching, concentrating on attacking Stan's garden boot. Stan grinned and played with the cat like a child. In the end, adeptly, and as if he were used to knowing when to step out of the fight, he removed his boot.

The cat stood up, walked away a few paces with a glowering dignity then sat in obsidian silence, observing another landscape.

Coming into the house later, Stan almost tripped over what had seemed, at first, a sprinkling of errant light. Instead it was one of the kittens.

Stan swore.

Molly, appearing with a tea towel in her hand, leant round the side of the kitchen wall.

'Be careful, Gabrielle, where you put the kittens. You can't let your grandfather trip and fall.'

Gabrielle, newly experienced in being part of the ménage, carried one of the little twisting bundles, and offered it with both hands to her grandfather.

'For you,' she said simply.

Stan gazed down into the child's face. There was an almost indecent degree of trust there. Gabrielle's blue eyes were frank. She was offering love. Her gift.

From the kitchen came Molly's voice.

'We can't keep the kittens, Gabrielle. They belong to someone else. Besides, we already have a cat.'

There was a tiny pause here, wherein Gabrielle looked up into her grandfather's face. The kitten had struggled out of his grasp, sprinted up Stan's arm and was now standing arched on Stan's shoulders. It seemed to survey its surroundings with élan. Then it rubbed itself against Stan's jaw. Only the child could see the almost helpless look of delight which swamped the old man's features.

'Gabrielle?' It was Molly from the kitchen. 'Don't annoy your grandpa.'

They were walking, a ragtag collection from house to house round the park. Molly was the one who knocked upon the doors. It was she who led the deputation who crowded round the doorstep on the rare occasion someone actually opened the door.

'I'm sorry to disturb you at this time of year . . .' she always began, curtseying to the proprieties, 'but we've found two kittens abandoned in the park.'

'They were lost,' Gabrielle almost always burst in. She was both proud and wanting to make the facts clear and known.

'Do you know who they might belong to?'

Nobody did. If people were feeling at a loose end, this led to long skeins of hypothesising. Perhaps the owners had gone away and left a neighbour's child to feed them? The child might have forgotten, or got bored. The kittens had collars, which certainly indicated they weren't wild. Most people said they had been busy 'at this time of year', so they hadn't noticed.

'Of course,' chimed in Molly, wanting to show she understood the nature of family priorities at this time of year.

Occasionally sullen children were separated from new toys, only to deliver the information that they too had not been in the park. These children gazed across an ocean of space towards Gabrielle, who tried to intimate to them by a special relaxation of her body that she would be pleased to join them in any games they might have on offer.

No offers were made.

Finally they reached the last house in the street. Its front door was wide open, disclosing a view of the back yard.

Molly knocked.

Down a passageway she saw a Turkish rug askew on a polished wood floor. There was a telephone, left off its cradle, as if someone had hurriedly gone away to look for something. Out the back door, she saw a bike, upside down, its wheel whirring.

She knocked again, calling out, in a lively sprinkle of sound, 'yoo-hoo'. The child imitated her, joyously. They all looked at each other, listened intently — then laughed.

Into this lovely — because so unusual — halo of sound, stepped a young man. He was wearing almost embarassingly small shorts (which Penny saw he filled to a pleasing degree). Apart from this he was 'as naked as the day he was born' as Molly said to herself, tut-tutting. He was lean, brown, with a flick of sun-whitened hair falling on his forehead.

'Hi there,' he said, 'I'm sorry I don't want . . .' He thought they were going door-to-door.

Penny spoke. 'My daughter —'

'I found two kittens up a tree.' Gabrielle spoke as if she had won something.

'Up a tree? Grey?' the young man said. 'With collars?'

'Yes.' Penny and Molly — unusually — spoke with one voice.

'They've been in the park since — well, I think the day before Christmas.'

'For —' Penny counted backwards, '— six days?'

The young man shrugged.

'I guess someone dumped them. You know. Bought for Christmas. Family goes away. Nobody wants them. Dumped.'

Molly felt tears in her eyes.

How could the world be so cruel? How could people be so thoughtless? Her gaze swang past Penny who, she noted, was talking to the young man in more detail.

'Aren't they anybody's?' Gabrielle thought to ask. To clarify.

'You mean they were left on their own, without food?' Molly found herself crying out. 'To fend for themselves? To find a way of surviving?'

The young man, no stranger to the concept of Darwinian struggle, shrugged again. 'Ring the SPCA,' he said. 'Though at this time of year it amounts to a death warrant.'

He smiled sunnily and closed the door.

'Can't you, Grandpa, keep him?'

Molly reached down and plucked the kitten off the old man's trousered thigh. The kitten tried to attach its claws into the fabric, and one claw stuck. He hung on, mewling in alarm.

'Leave him,' Stan ordered.

Molly dropped the kitten a little too abruptly. The kitten steadied itself on the mountain ledge of the old man's thigh and stared airily about. It seemed to assume ownership just a little too easily.

'What about Blacky?'

Molly turned her back. She was putting a tablecloth on the table.

Stan's hand felt down for the kitten and it almost instantly broke out into a ferocious and needy purr.

'We can't afford another cat.' This was Molly again, glancing over at her husband. 'One is enough.'

'I'll pay for the new cat,' Stan said to Molly as they lay in bed that night. This was so unusual that Molly did not at first say anything. Then she said, more caustically than she intended, 'You will, will you?'

Stan said nothing, but let out a long sigh then turned away from her. She rolled towards him and looked over at him.

'What about Blacky?' she said at last, no longer certain if he was awake. Stan was silent for a long while then, as if he had solved a philosophical conundrum which had required intense meditation, he murmured his philosophy in life: 'He'll get used to it.'

The next-door neighbour was looking for a cat. They would take one of the kittens. And Molly and Stan, at Gabrielle's behest, would take the remaining kitten — the one who had taken, almost limpet-like, to Stan.

Molly had witnessed Blacky's coming to terms with the kitten. Blacky had walked towards it grandly, as a duchess towards the most nervous debutante of the season. He had sniffed the kitten. Then he had turned away.

During feeding times, Molly observed that the kitten, called imaginatively 'Smoko', waited for Blacky to begin eating. Only after the older cat had begun, the younger male edged towards the food and began to eat in earnest. This was the only time the two animals ever came near each other. Once Molly saw Blacky reach out and, with an admonishing paw, bat the younger cat on the nose. His claws, she noted, were not out. The older cat pretended, or actually was, beyond caring about the younger cat's presence. They both had zones of the garden that were their own — Blacky reserving the best spots for himself — the lovely powdery dryness of the vegetable-garden soil to bask in the late afternoon sun — the shade beneath the grapevine in high summer because it caught a cooling draft — the spot right in front of the heater, in winter. But if this were so, Smoko got his 'father's' thigh, and reserved for himself a seat at the back of the stalls, near the heater. The new cat was awkward, clumsy; often, when walking across a table top, would overturn a vase. At times like this the older cat would seem to listen, a silent smile upon his mask-like face.

Gabrielle and Penny had long returned to America. Molly and Stan spoke of the new cat as 'Gabrielle's kitten', maintaining this fiction over the years, even as Gabrielle grew to be no longer a child, and in fact become a young woman.

One winter, towards the last, just as summer seemed about to call, Blacky died. As if following his faithful cat into the underworld, Stan faded away. His final breath had the soundlessness, the tact, of a cat's paw lifted from the soil.

Molly was alone. Apart from 'Gabrielle's kitten'. He was by now a young adult cat. But he had attached to him by now the almost invisible lustre of the sentences Molly and Stan had parsed by each other. It was through this cat that they had managed to express their affection, their need for companionship, for warmth — for language itself.

Many years later, Smoko himself had to be put down. This

unleashed in Molly an almost unreasoning torrent of grief. She realised it was out of scale and that, in mourning the cat, she was mourning much that she had never been able to articulate to herself — Stan, the impasse of their marriage, the alienation of her daughter — the loss of Ada, the woman she had loved so keenly during the war. She was cleansed by these emotions.

This was a gift from the death of her cat.

Molly hesitated to let Gabrielle know. She thought that Gabrielle would probably have no memory now of finding the kittens. But she was driven by the dying impulse of grief. She wished to reach out.

So Molly got out a pad. Penny had said to her that she wouldn't write letters till Molly got email. Molly was now eighty-two. She would not get email. Every so often she and Penny spoke on the phone. Penny seemed eager to talk to her now. Molly had the strange sense that she now had something Penny wanted: Penny came home each Christmas and spent it with Molly. So much older now, they were less enemies than old allies who had gone through a now long-forgotten civil war in which each family had known heartache, sorrow, death.

Penny told Molly that she kept Gabrielle up to date with Smoko's progress. Molly, who had the briefest outline of her granddaughter's almost unimaginably free life — she was a scientist in Houston — felt certain that Gabrielle would not be particularly interested. Perhaps she received it as some quaint curiosity, like Vegemite sandwiches, or maybe she even saw her grandmother's relationship to the cat as the very soul of pathos.

Yet in the end, Molly felt this was as much as she had ever

had with Gabrielle — those few moments of discovery of the cat. So now she got out her Croxley pad, and smoothed down the pages. She took up her Biro, nibbled the end and thought for a moment. She remembered from her youth a letter from her own grandmother and, knowing it to be antiquated yet apposite, she set the words down for her own granddaughter to marvel at.

'My dear Gabrielle,' she began.

OWEN MARSHALL

Thinking of Bagheera

'You don't much care for pets, I know,' says my neighbour. She smiles bleakly across the patio, and sips my Christmas sherry. She is pleased to be able to categorise me so utterly. It won't do to try to tell her of Bagheera, though what she says brings him back to me.

The cat was not even mine, but had been bought for my younger sisters. They soon excluded him from their affections, however. My sisters preferred those possessions which could be dominated. Compliant dolls who would accept the twisting of their arms and legs, and easily cleaned, bright, plastic toys. The cat went away a lot, and had for them a disconcerting smell of life and muscle.

My father named the cat Bagheera. My father had a predilection for literary allusion, to use his own phrase. Not that I heard him use it about himself. He was referring to Mr McIntyre, his deputy. I remember my father talking about Mr McIntyre to Mum; pausing to preface his remarks with a disparaging smile, and saying that Mr McIntyre had a predilection for literary allusion. I caught the tone although I couldn't understand the words. There was blossom on the ground that evening, for as he said it I looked out to the fruit trees, and saw the blossom blowing on the ground. Pink, apricot blossom, some lying amid the gravel of the drive, a fading tint towards the garage.

In the evening Bagheera and I would go for a walk. We agreed on equality in our friendship. We would maintain a general direction, but take our individual digressions. In the jungle of the potato rows or sweet corn I would hide, waiting for him to find me, and rub his round head against my face.

The cat brought trophies to the broad windowsill of my bedroom. Thrush wings, fledglings, mice and once a pukeko chick. My father hated the mess. He always drove the cat from the window when he saw it there. Yet often at night, waking briefly, I would look to the window and Bagheera would be there, a darker shape against the sky, his eyes at full stretch in the dusk. I was the only one in the family who could whistle him. It was a loyalty I would sometimes abuse just to impress my friends. Within a minute or two he would appear, springing suddenly from the roof of the sheds, or gliding from beneath the redcurrant bushes at the bottom of the garden. Beauty is not as common in this world as the claims that are made for it. But Bagheera's black hide flowed like deep water, and his indolent grace masked speed and strength. At times I would put my face right up to him to destroy perspective, and imagine him a full-size panther, see the broad expanse of his velvet nose, and his awesome Colgate smile.

In December Bagheera got sick. For three days he didn't come despite my whistling. We were having an end-of-term pageant at school and I was a wise man from the East, so I didn't have much time to look for him. But the day after we broke up, I heard Bagheera under the house. I talked to him for more than an hour, and he crawled bit by bit towards me, yet not close enough to touch. I hated to see him. He had scabs along his chin, his breathing made a sound like the sucking of a straw at the bottom of a fizz bottle. He wouldn't eat anything and just lapped weakly at the water I brought, before he backed laboriously again into the darkness under the house.

Each time I looked, his eyes would be blazing there, more fiery as his sickness grew, as if they consumed his substance.

My father decided to take Bagheera to the vet. He brought out Grandad's walking stick and said that he'd hook the cat out after I called him within reach. How easily the cat would normally have avoided such a plan. My father pinned Bagheera down, and tried to drag him closer. Bagheera rolled and gasped before he managed to free himself and crept back among the low piles. He knocked an empty tin as he went. It was the tin from the pears I had stolen after being strapped by my father for fishing in my best clothes.

When the walking stick failed, my father lost interest in the cat. He had given him his chance and after that he put the matter out of his mind. My father possessed a very disciplined mind. I couldn't forget, though, for Bagheera had become my cat. At night I would look sometimes to the window, but his calm presence was never there, and instead I kept thinking of his eyes in the perpetual darkness beneath the house. Beseeching eyes that waited for me to fulfil the obligation of our friendship.

I asked my father to shoot Bagheera. To put him out of his misery, I said. It was a common-enough expression, but my father had no conception of misery in others. I imagine he saw it, in regard to people at least, as the result of incompetence, or lack of drive. But I kept on at him. I said that Bagheera might spread infection to my sisters, or die under the house and cause a smell in the guest rooms. These considerations, which required no empathy, seemed to impress my father. He refused to fire under the house, though, he said. I'd have to coax Bagheera out where he could get a safe shot. He wasn't supposed to shoot at all within the borough limits, he said. At the time I didn't fully realise the irony of needing my father to kill Bagheera. I was the only possible go-between.

My father came out late in the afternoon, and stood with the rifle in the shade of the grapevine trellis, waiting for me to call Bagheera out. I felt the hot sun, unaccustomed on the back of my knees as I lay down. It was about the time that Bagheera and I would often take our walk, and I called him with all the urgency and need that I could gather. Even the pet names I used, even those, with the sensitivity of boyhood and my father standing there, for I would spare nothing in my friendship. Bagheera came gradually, his black fur dingy with the dust of the foundations, and the corruption within himself. I could hear his breathing, the straw sucking and spluttering, I could see his blazing eyes level with my own. To get him to quit the piles, and move into the light, was the hardest thing. I was aware of my father's impatience and adult discomfort with the situation.

'Move away from it,' he said, when Bagheera was at the verandah steps and trembling by the saucer of water. My father raised the .22, with which he never missed. No Poona colonel could have shown a greater sureness of aim. My sisters grouped at the study window to watch, their interest in the cat temporarily renewed by the oddity of his death.

The shot was not loud, a compressed, hissing sound.

Bagheera arched into the air, grace and panther for a last time, and sped away across the lawn into the garden. Just for one moment he raced ahead of death, just for one moment left death behind, with a defiance which stopped my breathing with its triumph. 'I wouldn't think anyone heard the shot at all,' said my father with satisfaction. The saucer lay undisturbed, and beside it one gout of purple blood. Don't tell me it wasn't purple, for I see it still, opalescent blood beside the freshly torn white wood the bullet dug in the verandah boards.

I didn't go to find the body among the currant bushes. Instead I went and lay hidden in the old compost heap, with the large, rasping pumpkin leaves to shade me, and the slaters questing back and forth, wondering why they'd been disturbed. My father and mother walked down by the hedge and I heard my father talking of Bagheera and me. 'I find it hard to understand,' he said. 'He seemed determined to have it shot. Sat there for ages cajoling it out to be shot. And after the attachment he seemed to have for it, too. He's a funny lad, Mary. Why couldn't he leave the wretched thing alone?' My father's voice had a tone of mixed indignation and revulsion, as if someone had been sick on the car seat, or one of his employees had broken down and cried. But I remembered Bagheera's release across the lawn, and thought it all worthwhile. He'd done his dash all right.

I lay in the evening warmth, and watched a pumpkin flower only inches from my face. Its image was distorted in the flickering light and shade beneath the leaves. The gaping, yellow mouth and slender stamen nodded and rolled like a processional Chinese dragon: the ones they have at weddings, and funerals.

VIVIENNE PLUMB

The Cinematic Experience

In the movies men and women on bicycles in the spring always means sex. If he takes his hat off, he is either being polite, or he means to stay. If she takes her shoes off, it's either sex or a comedy. A cat will indicate a tedious storyline. Something is about to happen. Like a fish bone caught in its throat. The appearance of a kitten is the same. But worse. The removal of clothes will indicate either sex or a hospital scene. Or possibly sex in a hospital. Hospitals are a big clue that someone will die, unless it is a comedy. A walk in the park is never that straightforward. Children are used in the script to hear voices, see ghosts, become lost, scream, or to tap dance. Babies ditto, but double all of the above.

GARY LANGFORD

The Couple Who Barbecue Cats

Around the same time that the couple's daughter, Marlene, runs away, the cats on the hills begin to go missing. The first cat to disappear is Marlene's beloved Orlando, large of build with eyes that seem suspicious of everyone but her. The couple purchase a portable barbecue, black and shaped like a flying saucer. The husband attends a cooking workshop, becoming an expert in meat-based cuisine, while his wife is especially proud of her chilli sauce, which has a sharp bite to it. 'Produced from all-local ingredients,' she tells guests with a smile.

'Just like the meat,' adds the husband.

The couple laughs delightedly, and their laugher spreads to the guests who feel cheered up.

The couple are unsurprised by Marlene's disappearance. She was always bound for trouble; smoking at ten, drinking spirits at thirteen, arrested twice for possession of cocaine. On the first occasion, the couple was told that Marlene was found with coke in her handbag.

'What's wrong with that?' asked the husband.

'Too much sugar,' reflected his wife. 'She's always been, like the young are, prey to advertising.' Cocaine had hardly been heard of in the city in those days.

'We've brought her up as best we could,' said the husband.

'What can you do?' asked the wife, when they were told the coke in their daughter's handbag was *not* a soft drink.

The only good thing about Marlene was her devotion to cats. For years she tried to persuade them to get more cats, but the couple refused to, disliking the animals. One cat was one too many; they wouldn't indulge her anymore. Orlando knew this, seldom going near them, but was extremely devoted to Marlene, who cried for days when Orlando's first kittens were given away. (This was what the couple told her, although the kittens were packed into a sack and tossed off the bridge into the river.)

Marlene was delighted that Orlando was female, not male as had previously been thought. Female cats bothered the couple even more. Not long after the kittens, they had Orlando desexed at the vet when their daughter was away. Marlene said she would never forgive them. And she didn't, being a girl fierce in her passions, particularly as her passion was cats.

Marlene had cats on her wallpaper, cats on her clothes, and a cat tattooed on her left buttock, which men took bets on stroking without being bitten. They found that pretending to like cats increased her libido and their chances of removing her cat clothes — something they all wanted to do — let alone getting between her cat thighs.

She was a cat males wanted to stroke and get purring, a beautiful cat with green eyes. These eyes attracted, or bothered, most people. Eyes of spiritual value, men from other cultures believed, even if they prayed for sexual rather than spiritual revelation.

There were a growing number of occasions when people

said she looked like a cat. Perhaps it was the way her long nails were shaped like claws. Perhaps it was the few men who got into bed with her without being clawed, saying she purred rather than made sounds of orgasm. Perhaps it was simply those large green eyes, which gazed unfathomably, or the way she would curl up in a chair, rather than sit.

The bond between Marlene and Orlando was a powerful one. Nobody was shocked that, when Marlene ran away from home, Orlando went missing. It was as if he had packed up and gone in search of her. This was how the couple explained it to anyone who asked, nodding wisely to each other and sighing.

The couple live on the hills overlooking the Heathcote and Avon River estuaries. They started a family in their late thirties so they could afford to live there. They believed in planning. Neighbours sympathised with them over the trouble Marlene brought into their lives, whether it was with the police, or the many males who knocked on doors, asking where sexy Marlene was.

Once the husband upset his wife by firmly replying, 'We don't have women like that up here.'

Nobody on the hills misses Marlene when she runs away, but neighbours do begin to miss their cats: black cats, tabby cats, marmalade cats, fat cats, thin cats, lords, ladies and runts.

A cloud lifts from the couple's spirits. They are the first to sympathise with others when their cats disappear — they know all about it.

'What you need is a good barbecue,' says the husband.

'Not that you can ever replace a beloved moggy,' adds the wife, sighing. 'We remember when poor Orlando vanished. A barbecue helped us tremendously.'

'Whoever's doing this should be whipped.' The husband frowns.

And barbecued.' The wife nods.

Such comments are accepted gratefully. People develop a new appreciation of the couple.

There follow many barbecues, each featuring tender meat with special sauce. Guests enthuse over the magnificent dishes, convinced they are unique, and forget the view as they try to discover how they are created.

'Cooks never give away their secrets,' says the husband.

'Not if they want to go on cooking,' adds the wife.

The cats are taken at random. The only things they have in common are being well fed, well looked-after and that they live on the hills overlooking the coast. They are cats sunning themselves under small citrus trees, the presence of which defies the efforts of the nor'westers, which blow across the plains to remove them. They are cats living and dying on a better diet than many humans in the city below. Each cat vanishes in the night, soundlessly, not a miaow to be heard, as if called away, enticed by parties unknown. Rumours abound. The cats are being taken for their fur, which is sold overseas. The cats are being used in Asian restaurants in the city. A few of the locals go to check these restaurants out, miaows in their ears as the food approaches.

At Sumner, there is only one road into the suburb, or village as locals like to call it, unless you come from the other direction, over the hills. Most locals like to look down on the city twinkling in the distance at night, as it's blamed for all the missing cats. The city drives out to Sumner on Sundays, especially in summer. Someone must have seen all the beautiful cats, and decided to market them in one form or another. One of the drunken locals suggests that all cars going back across thc causeway be searched. For a moment he is listened to, until he adds, 'By cats.'

Late summer. Sixty-eight cats have disappeared. Even the couple is worried so many have gone from the hills — far more than they have barbecued. People insist the police do something so a young policeman is sent up from the city for a week, parading around the hills in uniform. He finds nothing but gets a good suntan, writing in his report: *There must be a lot of cats up here if the locals think most are missing. I saw dozens of them, often together, following me. Sounds crazy but every time I turned around a cat was staring at me from a tree, or sitting on a rock with impenetrable eyes set on me. Cats are creepy.*

His report is read, then filed.

The final barbecue is after two cats owned by the people next door to the couple go missing. They are large, overfed cats that pant as they waddle down the path, let alone descend to Mulgan's Track on a big adventure. This Sunday-afternoon barbecue is held on the couple's verandah, which directly overlooks the estuary. They are so hospitable that the guests cheer up and almost forget their cats are missing.

'Have some more,' says the wife when the first helping is scoffed down.

'The meat's delicious. What is it?'

'We like to surprise people,' explains the husband. 'Life doesn't have enough surprises.'

'It has too many,' replies one of the guests, staring down at the water below, shimmering on a hot afternoon. 'Our cats,' he begins, then stops as if he has seen them rowing across the estuary.

'Are delicious,' agrees the husband.

'Pardon?' asks the guest, wondering if he has heard this correctly.

'It's all in the sauce,' reflects the wife.

'And the meat, dear,' argues the husband. 'We decided *that* after Orlando. Every meal is a question of balance and personal reflection.'

'Like life.' The wife nods.

The guests stare at each other, then at their plates, then back at each other. Neither can bring themselves to ask the question on both their lips.

'This may sound callous,' says the husband cheerfully, 'but these things often turn out for the best. Look at us, things have never been better since we rid ourselves of Orlando.'

'Well said, dear,' agrees the wife. Not long after this, their guests excuse themselves, returning home, convinced they have just eaten their pets.

Later that night, the couple goes for a walk as they usually do, wearing dark clothes and soft-soled shoes, carrying a can of cat food. This is their last hunt for cats. Peculiar things are happening on the hills at night. The couple has barbecued over a dozen cats, all from houses near theirs. Now they can sit on their verandah without a cat in sight. They don't understand why all these other cats are disappearing, joking to each other, 'There's a copycat about.' Yet they are concerned. They sense they are being followed on their night-walks, but they whip around to find that nobody is there.

Nonetheless, the couple is convinced something *is* there. Once they would have laughed at such an idea, but not any more. Whoever is following them is even lighter on his feet than they are.

The couple walks further up the hill until the road flattens out, knowing this is a hunting ground for cats, due to earlier research for their cat barbecues. Again, they have that uncomfortable feeling they are being watched. The husband hurriedly opens the can of cat food, frowning slightly. It is the wife who has insisted they hunt for another cat, the mystery ingredient in her tasty sauces. Each time they go out to search increases their chances of being caught, especially as this is the first time they have moved away from near their house, not for research, but for the kill. Who would suspect them? Still, the husband reminds himself to talk to his wife about ending the cat-hunt. Tonight is our last cat, he tells himself firmly.

The couple has discovered that the ads on television are correct. If you tap a spoon on the tin can of food, sooner or later a cat will appear, licking its lips, while you are licking yours. Greed wins out over danger. They are surprised when nothing happens, tapping the can again. Still nothing.

The husbands tells the wife to wait there, turns back up the road to where he glimpsed a cat earlier, leaving the can with her.

She sits down on some steps leading up to the house immediately above them. Out of curiosity she tastes the cat food, wrinkling her face in disgust, wondering how cats can eat such horrible food. If she were a cat she would insist on real meat. Like Marlene always gave Orlando. This was why Orlando tasted so rich and tender, the prime piece of all the cat meat they have eaten. How she loathed that cat. How she loved eating him.

There is movement in the bushes behind her.

Down the road, the husband pauses, sniffing the wind, a clean smell, glancing behind himself when he thinks he hears his wife calling. He listens, hearing only the sound of bushes stirring in the wind. The lights of the city glitter to the north and west. He has always enjoyed watching the city at night, and does so now. The plain of stars, he thinks, remembering how, when he was a child, he vowed that one day he would live on the hills, looking down on where he was born. *Swamp-city*, he calls it, and smiles,

The husband is still smiling as he feels something approaching softly from the side. Just for a moment he sees a huge cat out of the corner of his eye. Even more briefly, he recognises the cat, opening his mouth in shock. Before he can say anything, the cat is upon him, knocking the air out of his lungs as she strikes, paws on his chest as she tears his throat out with a few yanks of her carefully polished teeth. He is killed easily. If the cat is disappointed, she gives no sign.

Nor does she play with the body as cats usually do. She takes hold of one leg and drags him down the road.

Other cats are waiting in the bushes: black cats, tabby cats, marmalade cats, fat cats, thin cats, lords, ladies and runts. All are purring as the large cat, obviously the leader, drags the body into the centre of them, dropping it beside the one already there. She regards her following matter-of-factly, as if to say, 'Have as much as you like.' She steps backwards, letting the small cats begin feeding, then the larger ones after them. Some like the meat, others the warm blood. None of them like barbecue sauce.

The following morning, fifty-five cats return home, looking surprisingly well fed and content after their disappearance. Their owners make a great fuss of them, further surprised when the cats refuse to eat the bowls of meat that are placed in front of them. The cats disdainfully sniff the meat from cans, tails flicking backwards in discontent, turning and looking at their owners, licking their lips in anticipation. The owners stare at them, uncertain what the cats are waiting for, sighing as they bend down to pick up the cat food, thinking, You can't always predict how cats will behave.

If the couple were present on this day, they would have been pleased to know all missing cats are accounted for. Except Orlando, and the other barbecued cats. And, of course, Marlene.

STEPHANIE JOHNSON

Cat House

One night they went to a party alive with dancing doctors, which was held in a large new concrete-and-glass house on a cliff top, designed by Dan. That was why they'd been invited: one of the doctors had been a client. These particular doctors partied and drank as though they were at the end of exams, nineteen again, not professionals in their late thirties with mounting responsibilities and growing families — which Dan and Tess were too, almost. Until about eleven o'clock it seemed that every second woman in the room was pregnant, then they all melted away, leaving the party animals to get on with it.

In a basket under a table there was a real animal, a tall-boned, massive-faced cat called a Maine Coon which, although it may have enjoyed stalking seagulls along the cliff — it was easily big enough to catch one — was forced to live its life indoors. As Tessa put down her glass and picked up the cat, cuddling it to her, a creature the weight and size of a small two-year-old, they were joined by another guest. He was a garrulous Irish oncologist, who had recently arrived in Auckland. Originally he had trained in psychiatry, he told them, and went on with a story about a past patient, a man who believed that all the cats in Dublin were telling him to pee through letter boxes set in the front doors of houses. The man had obliged, opening the metal slots and pissing on the carpets of people's hallways. One day a particularly muscular letter-box flap sprang back and severed his penis.

The doctor had treated the man while he was recovering from surgery to save his life. It was a stitch-up job, not a re-attachment; the patient being too insane to relate details of what he had been doing before he was found slumped, bleeding on this particular front step, and the instrument that separated shaft from groin remaining surprisingly bloodless. The emergency services, therefore, were given no clue. Languishing on a rubber mat on the other side of the door in a puddle of pink pee, the penis remained undiscovered until the residents came home that evening and found it orphaned, anaemic as weisswurst.

'Incurable,' said the oncologist. 'A madman doomed to piss through a straw. At least now I cure people.'

At that moment a twenty-stone skin specialist given to wild manoeuvres on the dance floor crashed through a plate-glass panel and so caused a distraction and very shortly afterwards the end of the party. Tessa put the cat down and wove a little, as they went down the tiled steps towards the car.

'There were things I wanted to ask that doctor,' Tessa said on the way home, 'such as, why were the cats telling that guy to pee through people's front doors? Did they want him to mark the houses for them? Did they hold him in high esteem like an honorary tomcat? Had they lionised him?'

'The guy was nuts.' Dan swung his head round to look at her, appalled, and the car swerved.

'Lionised,' whispered Tess. 'Ha ha.'

'They weren't telling him anything. You know that.' Dan concentrated on the road.

'They might have been,' said Tess, folding her thin white hands in her lap and jutting her pointy chin. 'Cats are very mysterious creatures, which you could find out for yourself, if you'd take the antihistamine.'

'The guy was nuts,' Dan repeated. 'He was a total loon.'

'You don't understand,' Tess said. 'I feel sorry for you.'

She was silent then and Dan hoped she was remembering the stories he'd told her; the reason why it was that every time he saw a cat's sleek pelt basking on a sunny wall he imagined the particles of saliva stuck on the fur and contributing to the sheen. In his adolescence, having suffered through childhood a worsening allergic reaction to a succession of his sisters' cats, just the sight of one crossing the road was enough to start him itching and wheezing. Now he was less suggestible, but he hadn't had to live with one of the fish-breathed sacks of pus for years.

'Such a shame we can't have one of you,' Tessa had whispered into the Maine Coon's fur-filled auricle.

'You know you would never have to go into it,' Tessa said now, as Dan pointed the remote control at the garage door, and he knew without asking that she was talking about her idea for a cat house. She'd drawn up the plans herself on his old drawing board: a structure to fill most of their small back yard, to be furnished with climbing frames and nests, and fitted with transparent tubes running across the lawn that the cats could pass through, and so get an idea of sky and weather.

'Make sure you wash your hands before you come to bed,' Dan said as they went inside. 'I don't want to wake up covered in welts.'

'I've got something to show you,' she said. 'Mum gave it to me this afternoon.' Side by side in the marital bed they looked at the photograph. It was Tess at about thirteen, reclining on a blue sofa with a fat ginger cat on her stomach, eyes blissfully closed to her stroking hand. A black-and-white lay along the back rest and a third, long-haired and kitten-sized, lay curled in the open collar of her pyjamas. The dainty adolescent feet crossed on the rolled arm of the sofa were clad in bright pink slippers with feline faces, and tossed on the floor in the foreground there was a cat-shaped cushion. More arresting, Dan found, was the expression on Tessa's face; her innocent sensuality, the particular cast of her pretty lips and eyes. It was an expression he recognised and even now, after six years of marriage, would sometimes picture longingly at odd moments of his working day.

'Sweet Tess,' he said, his stroking hand travelling up her slender inner thigh and his mercifully still-attached penis beginning to wag.

'I'm out after work,' Tessa told him on Monday morning before she departed for her job, a middle-management position at a city corporate. 'I've got Rescue.'

At the local gym Dan went through his routine on the bench presses and treadmill, following on his circuit a tall, broad-beamed blonde, who reminded him of photographs of Russian peasants before the revolution. She looked like she could effortlessly bear twenty children and incubate any premature ones between her mighty breasts. He wondered if he was as removed from his instincts as the Maine Coon doubtless was. He'd chosen a woman with hips as narrow as a poodle's, the appetite of an ant and the panicked constitution of a coal-mine canary. She didn't even look fertile. Maybe it was time to pay a visit to a fertility specialist. He'd ask the cliff-top dweller for the name of the best.

Tessa waited on the comer, outside her building, watching the evening traffic halt by. It was cold and drizzly, a winter night drawing in fast, and she was glad of her thick parka and corduroy pants. Neatly folded into a carry-bag under her arm were her office clothes, the silk suit and high heels not suitable for crossing rough terrain, such as that of cemeteries, or beneath Grafton Bridge, or motorway flyovers. Why was Cheryl late? she wondered. Usually her patrol partner was prompt; sometimes the bright-yellow van with the battered plastic Garfield attached to the radiator was waiting for her when she came out of the lobby. Cheryl was plump and unmarried, with nine overfed cats, and very often, as she was treating Tessa to stories about them or showing her yet another envelope of cat-filled photographs, Tessa envied her her crowded bed.

Eventually, the rescue van came around the corner of Wellesley Street. Instead of Cheryl's bottle-blonde head in the cab, there was a man's ginger one. He had a ginger beard and orange jacket, and he looked familiar. It wasn't until Tessa climbed aboard that she recognised him. It was Kane, the Irish oncologist from the party.

'I thought you'd hate cats,' she said to him, after they'd got over their initial surprise at meeting again, 'after your story about that poor man in Dublin.'

'Not at all,' he said. 'Cats can be a very healing influence.'

'Do you need healing?' Tessa asked. It occurred to her suddenly that perhaps, as happens sometimes, the specialist had developed his own disease.

'Only as much as we all do,' he said. 'Less since I came to this country. It's important to keep the numbers down here, so we're doing good all round. Protecting the birdlife and sterilising the cats, or giving them a humane end.'

'Is that why you do it?' Tessa said, horrified. 'I don't think of anything but the cats themselves. Easing their pain, healing them. When you're out there, in the dark, hearing abandoned kittens crying for their vanished mothers, or finding a brave old warrior stinking with abscesses and filled with worms, well, you just . . . you just . . . you can't think about anything else other than them . . . their wellbeing,' she finished lamely. Wait until she told Cheryl about this guy. She wouldn't believe it. She'd tell headquarters.

'Don't get me wrong,' said Kane, turning off Symonds Street into St Martin's Lane, 'I've got three of my own. Look — Sphynxes. Very warm to the touch.'

Kane had opened his wallet and was showing her the picture, holding it out under a street lamp. Two hairless gargoyles with grey wrinkled skin curled together on a red velvet bedspread. They were the only breed Tessa didn't like — they didn't even look like cats. They looked as though they should live underground.

As they walked on Kane pulled out another photograph from behind the first and held it out under the light at the cemetery gate.

'And then there's Bono.'

Bono was the same colour as Kane, red and cream, a long-haired domestic, a common moggy. He was plump and old and Tessa thought his eyes looked sad.

'Came with me from Ireland. Did the quarantine and all. Not so sold on the new cats, but I missed him so when he was in the lockup. Saw these guys on eBay and had to have them. I think he understands . . .'

He was looking at the photograph of the Sphynxes again. Tessa took the lead and went through into the cemetery.

By the end of the night, just before ten, they'd fed a colony in the planting beside the North-western Motorway and another three in various parks; they'd caged and doped a juvenile torn with festering battle-wounds and rescued a young queen scarcely out of kittenhood with six kittens of her own. They'd cleared and set traps, humane cages with food inside. The trapped cats sometimes hissed at them from behind the bars as they lifted them into the van. At headquarters they bedded the poor creatures down and left their logbook and case notes on the table for the vet.

'Come home for a drink?' Kane said, as she rang for a taxi. 'I've got my car here — I'll give you a lift home afterwards.'

'I would like to meet Bono,' Tessa admitted.

'And the Sphynxes. People often disapprove of them — for no good reason. They're mysterious little creatures all right, with an interesting slant on the world.'

Kane lived on the third floor of a new apartment block with a balcony. It was a small flat, almost a bedsitter, with the red velvet bed she'd seen in the photograph separated from the sitting room only by a Chinese screen. On the wall was a black-and-white relief map of New Zealand with pins in various locales, she supposed to mark places Kane had visited. As they'd come in the hairless cats had sprung from where they were, coiled like lizards on a leather sofa, and mewed for food. Out on the balcony, solid and unyielding, his back to them, Bono sat on the other side of his cat door. While Kane poured two shots of Scotch, Tessa opened the sliding door and went out. She stroked Bono lightly after letting him sniff her hand. The cat resisted for a moment, going so far as to turn his fluid neck and nip her fingers. But she persisted with her caressing, undeterred, until he leaned into her, allowing her to pick him up and carry him into the room. She sat with him on the leather sofa the others had vacated. Their bony tails protruded around the kitchen cabinets, thrashing as they ate.

'Very clean,' Kane told her. 'Very suited to apartment living. Bono spends most of his time sitting on the balcony.'

'He hates it here,' Tessa said.

'Has he told you that already?' Kane said. He smiled, showing his very white teeth. 'He doesn't mince his words, that one.'

'It's obvious,' said Tessa.

'Have you got a garden?' Kane asked her. 'Room for one extra? In Dublin I lived in a terrace house, see, and he could go out and about.'

'Yes and no,' said Tessa, and she told him about Dan's allergy and how she couldn't in all fairness take a cat. She wondered if she should tell him about her cat house idea, but he might think that was silly and desperate. Instead she found herself absorbed in the spectacle of the two bald creatures leaping to their keeper's knee, purring and rubbing against one another, and Kane's eager fondling of their necks and ears, his coddling fingers massaging and rubbing their soft, leathery flanks. They were thin, lacking in muscle tone, like spoilt anorexic girls. Kane was clearly fascinated by them, his eyes shining, his head bent as if he was listening to secrets.

Bono settled on her own lap, facing her, purring loud and soft, rhythmically, then missing a beat, his fluffy tail against her legs, his heavy hairy warmth melting away the graveyard–motorway chill that had earlier seeped into her muscles, while her cosseting palm sleeked his back. The Scotch and night's work made her feel drowsy and since Kane was quiet, Tessa not given to small talk, and the sound of three cats purring soporific, her eyes began to close.

In the early hours of the morning she was dimly aware of a soft woollen rug being folded over her and Bono, who had remained with her, adjusting his position when she'd curled up on the wide cushion. Tessa opened her eyes to the oncologist bending to tuck the rug behind her shoulder, clad only in a t-shirt, as if he'd got out of bed especially to cover her in the coldest hours before dawn. As he raised his arms the shirt lifted, to reveal a froth of red pubic hair and nothing else. There was an absence. The observation so startled her half-dreaming mind that it propelled her back to deep sleep, borne on the swift wings of denial: she had imagined it.

It was perhaps only an hour later that she woke properly and gave Bono one final stroke and a whispered promise to come again soon, before she let herself quietly out of the flat.

'Where've you been?' Danny opened the door before she'd even got her key in the lock, 'I've been up all night worrying.

I was just about to ring the police. I thought something must've happened —'

'Shshsh,' said Tessa. 'It's all right.' She gave her husband a kiss, without touching him. She hadn't washed her hands yet. 'I went with one of the rescue people to see his cats and fell asleep on his sofa.'

Perhaps Tessa was ignorant of the fact that not one husband in history has believed that story from his wife: the story of another man's sofa and chaste sleep. Daniel's intelligence was insulted.

'Yeah, right,' he said, 'Of course you did.'

'I *did*!' Tessa told him about Bono and the Sphynx pair, but omitted to tell him that the man was the oncologist that they'd met at the party. Perhaps because of that omission she elaborated a little, to pad the story out, and told him that Bono had actually been given to her, but because her friend understood about allergies and was sympathetic to Dan, they'd made an arrangement for her to visit the cat daily. She thought Bono was a clever enough fellow to go for a walk on a lead, so she hoped she'd be able to show him around the Domain a little. She decided she would never pay any attention at all to the hairless cats so that Bono knew he was special to her.

Dan listened impatiently, though not angrily, and she could see all the cat details were convincing him. While he got ready to go to the gym she made herself coffee, and while she drank it, she decided she would not tell him about what she thought she had seen in the middle of the night. If she told Dan that, what she'd seen while Kane tucked the blanket around her and the sad old cat on her lap, then he'd be bound to try to stop her going to see him.

poems

Ursula Bethell

Garden-lion

O Michael, you are at once the enemy
and the chief ornament of our garden,
Scrambling up rose-posts, nibbling at nepeta,
Making your lair where tender plants should flourish
Or proudly couchant on a sun-warmed stone.
What do you do all night there,
When we seek our soft beds,
And you go off, old roisterer,
Away into the dark?
I think you play at leopards and panthers;
I think you wander on to foreign properties;
But on winter mornings you are a lost orphan
Pitifully wailing underneath our windows;
And in summer, by the open doorway,
You come in pad, pad, lazily to breakfast,
Plumy tail waving, with a fine swagger,
Like a drum-major, or a parish beadle,
Or a rich rajah, or the Grand Mogul.

Crisis

When Michael plays on a bidibid' patch,
And a crestfallen figure of fun
Approaches our portals furtively,
All hands muster and run
As if to a grass-fire, incontinently,
Down tools, hurry and run —
Seize him before his endeavours
To gloss the disaster have begun.
Though he bite and claw, half in fury
And half in gratified fun,
We most gently and delicately
The embedded burrs one by one
Disengage from his opulent vesture
Till the morning hours have run.
All my work antedated!
All our duties undone!
Because great Michael rolled heedlessly
On a bidibidi patch in the sun!

Ah, Michael, year by year the same catastrophe;
Yearly these old incorrigible capers;
Yearly must we undo the work of atavistic vagrancy;
Because Dame Nature has withheld from you, old
blunderer
(But not from us, the bludgeoned and belaboured!),
The deep incisive doctrines of experience.

Admonition

Now, Michael, understand me. Be attentive.

The hedgehogs are my very good friends;
So are the lizards, basking in the sun;
Of the bush-warblers I will say nothing —
There you are fanatical and will not listen,
So we must differ (the little birds have wings).
But take heed that we find no tailless lizards:
Know that the rockwalls are reserved for lizards;
And you shall not frighten hedgehogs in the dark;
Confine, Michael, your hostilities to rabbits,
The neighbour's dog, mice (if any), or a rat.

Or those phantom creatures in the undergrowth,
Creaking, rustling, crawling before daybreak,
Making your eyes burn and your fur tingle,
When our garden turns into a strange jungle,
An old cat-ghostly forest, an immemorial hunting-
ground,
So wild, so still, so dangerous
Before the break of day.

JANET CHARMAN

lives and lives
— the overlap cats

awoken with
the soft fall shock
of a cat
on the outside sill

she sleeps through
the mown lawn afternoons
— when pressed
gives her unravelling stretch
for my scratch

around my feet
insisting
but not wanting to eat
— i open the door
to a warmer room
and she's gone

sorrow of mine
descending in a stroke
she puts up with it
for a bit
and walks off

we dress his wounds
you hold his head
while i swab
he doesn't fight

idiotic with cobweb
and worrying at
his damp coat
— licked along till it's
scent secured

knows not to
soil inside
yet her daughter kitten's
grown and forgotten

decked rats
endangered species
little sweeties

W. H. OLIVER

Cat

Not the complete animal?
Sufficiently so, having contrived
to resist the operation.
Two could not persuade him
into the box without loss of blood.
Three good legs, one, left rear,
awkward since he was hit by a car,
get him about well enough,
straight up a cabbage tree
with a noise like tearing paper
and quick as a flash to a meal.
Lately he has been away nights
and sometimes all day lying up
I suppose exhausted. Front on
he is like a strong triumphal arch
topped by a broad kingly head
glowing dark gold in the sun.
Curled up by the heater
his bad leg is tucked away
he looks complete as he is
apart from a bit of one ear,
no great loss, rather
a distinction, an emblem.

BRIAN TURNER

Morning Delivery

A nest of grey feathers on the doorstep,
one undespotic eye, a dull beak,
three spots of dried blood,

and the cat under the house, resting.
And the sun sizing us up
sitting on the rim of the long ridge

that rises out of the bay.

cats I have known

JEFFREY MASSON

Extract from 'Love'

To most of us, the most beautiful word in any language is our own name spoken to us with love by somebody we love back. Cats are no exception. It is strange, when you think about it, that cats love to hear us repeat their name, but they do. Cats know their name of course; they know that the name we speak is only for them — their very own, singular name. They know, too, that when we say it with love, as we often do, we are saying something special to them. This gives them enormous pleasure. What is the nature of that pleasure? Why would these solitary animals be driven to ecstasy by the sound of their own name? What are they hearing?

If you ask people who live with cats (I do this all the time) what their cat likes best about them, the first response is invariably something to do with material life. I asked the novelist Stephanie Johnson what her cat loved in her, and she said, 'I know how to open the fridge door, and all he ever does, I swear, is stare at that door. If you were to look into his mind, you would see a white oblong shape, strangely resembling our family fridge.' If a cat's life is reduced to sleeping and eating, then clearly the cat will think about this all the time. However, a cat may love you for many different things, some of them material, some of them intangible, some of them obvious, some obscure. We should not expect to exhaust the list any time soon. Even if we could ask them, they might not be able to enumerate all the ways they love us.

Nobody who lives with cats would believe they are indifferent to humans. Nevertheless, some hard-nosed scientists are not convinced that cats feel love and affection. In the nineteenth century, Nathaniel Southgate Shaler, dean of science at Harvard, a great foe of the cat and lover of evidence, said, 'I have been unable to find any authenticated instances which go to show the existence in cats of any real love for their masters.' We might argue endlessly about what exactly an authenticated instance would be, but of cat love for humans there are no end to stories, testimonies, and direct observations. Among the best is an account by Frances and Richard Lockridge, mystery-story writers (their popular North tales first appeared in *The New Yorker* in 1936), in their invaluable book *Cats and People* (first published in 1950 and still one of the best books ever written about cats), where they write about their beloved Pammy. When Richard was absent during part of World War II, 'Pammy was brokenhearted — one does not like to use terms so extreme, but other terms are inadequate. The bottom dropped out of Pammy's life.' What is the evidence?

She would go to the door of the small room where Richard always was. She knew that he was not there and, after looking into the room, she would 'raise her head and give a small, hopeless cry.' She would turn away and wander the apartment restlessly, returning again and again to the room, only to find it empty. If she heard the front door open, she was all ears, but she would know instantly from the footsteps that it was the wrong sound, and she would cry and wander again.

The Lockridges write, 'But if, during those weeks, she did

not feel deeply the loss of someone she loved, then the actions of cats and men make no sense at all, and the words we use have no meaning.' As I was writing these lines, Minnalouche was sitting perched on the top of my computer monitor. She looked down at my fingers racing across the keyboard, following their movement. Then she glanced up at my face and blinked. I blinked back, and that gesture alone (one of friendship in cat language, indicating that one has no predatory intent) so delighted her that she began to purr loudly. I had not petted her; it was the mere *idea* of my friendship that had pleased her so. The Lockridges write of their Siamese cat, Martini, 'When she blinks a little, gently, as we speak her name, it would be easy to think that there is a kind of adoration in her mind.'

Because cats lack a protective antibacterial enzyme in their tears (lysozyme — humans and most other animals have it), they can blink as infrequently as once in five minutes. (It is hard to believe that blinking exposes the eyes of domestic cats to more bacteria than those of a wild cat, who would not have to blink in a friendly matter except under unusual circumstances, but perhaps it is so; one of the disadvantages of domestication for cats.) If cats blink rarely, do they do so only when they want to suggest friendly feelings? The medieval church fathers thought it was evil for a cat to stare at you and not blink. Humans are more like the social dog in this respect, and respond to a stare with aggression. My cats stare out of affection. They also signal their lack of hostility by deliberately blinking from time to time, perhaps afraid I will misunderstand. Megala is a frequent blinker. He has also developed a blocked tear duct about which little can be done medically. Are the two connected?

Cats look away or blink when feeling friendly. Dogs, under similar conditions, close their eyes slightly. Humans, according to James Serpell, director of the Center for the Interaction of Animals and Society, at the University of Pennsylvania, are probably the only mammal to use eye-to-eye contact as a means of expressing intimacy (in monkeys, dogs and cats, it conveys hostility). This probably goes back to the nursing dyad, where the infant gazes, with something approaching love, into the eyes of the mother. When petted, cats will look up at their companions with a look we interpret — correctly, I believe — as adoration.

Like most cats, mine do not like rain. Yet when Leila, Ilan, Manu and I walk up the hill in the evening in the rain, such is the cats' devotion that they come with us. I could not quite credit it the first time it happened, but they do it often enough now to have convinced me that their own comfort is secondary to them; first comes the desire to be with us. The love could be for us, for the adventure, for the variety, but it is beyond question that the cats are doing something because they *want to,* because they derive pleasure from it. Moreover, since they walk in the rain only when we are there, never alone, the love of our companionship must be a strong component of their pleasure.

I believe not only that cats think about us on a fairly regular basis, but also that they can read our intentions or, deeper still, our true feelings about them. A woman I know, mad about cats, took one look at Yossie and suffered a *coup de foudre.* She got down on all fours and cooed to him. Yossie looked stunned: ran over, rubbed noses, then began the most shameless display of requited love — 'Yes, oh yes, me too, I feel just as you do,

I am yours forever.' It was unmistakable. Now, Yossie clearly likes me; he does more than tolerate me, but he is not wild about me. He was instantly wild about her. Why? Because he read her so clearly. Her love for him was unconditional, or so it must have appeared to Yossie. Maybe he sees in me some hesitation, some uncertainty about his 'character', about how trustworthy he is with children, which does indeed make me hold back total devotion to him.

It still seems to me, though, that the cats like one another more than they like me; they never groom me as they do each other. Today I brought Moko back from the vet, where he was treated for ear mites, and Miki cleaned out his ear with his tongue while Moko purred. If cats have no other cat, then they tend to treat us as cats and will groom us but, given a choice, they prefer their own kind. Not surprising, really. The surprise is that they like us as much as they do, especially since cats rarely like other animals at all, except for dogs. Cats can be very close to dogs, so close that they become inseparable companions, and many people have told me that when their dog dies, their cat goes into mourning. When I had dogs and cats together, they would often set off on adventures with each other. Cats can like a rabbit or even a mouse, but they will rarely bond in the same deep way with those animals as they do with us and sometimes with dogs. What is it that cats, humans and dogs have in common? Our devotion to love.

What about cats who seem to like no other cat? There are cats who resent the intrusion of any new cat into their home (which has become their territory); they disapprove of affection shown to a strange and needy animal, and they want all the food, all the attention, and all the love for themselves. Many people have only one cat in their home because they have been convinced, by experience or by mythology, that cats prefer it that way. I do not believe it is true (though I wonder why my cats sniff at me so intensely when I have been out cavorting with strange cats). My five cats are not related and came to us at different times, yet four of the five are good friends. They sleep together, eat together, play together, and take walks together. Here is the key: if cats are living in stressful conditions, where there is not enough food or not enough stimulation, they may well resent the presence of other cats who take away these vital requirements. Even feral cats act quite differently according to whether there is plenty of food or whether they are really on their own. When there is plenty of food, the cats tend to not only be tolerant of one another, but actually form friendships. I would not say that most domestic cats are loners, only that they evolved to be loners and can easily revert to it.

In a short story 'Cats', by the writer Robley Wilson Jr., a woman explains to her new beau, a therapist, that she has two cats who 'think they are brothers. It can't do any harm if I let them go on thinking so, can it?' He responds stiffly, 'It's all right to be silly over animals, so long as you know you're being silly.' Bad answer. He is soon history, and at the end of the story, the woman watches her cats moving down her long driveway and she suddenly feels 'the welling-up of emotions she hadn't known since the days when her sons went off to school together. *That's love,* she told herself. *There's nothing foolish about love.*' It is a wonderful phrase, that there is nothing silly about love, whether expressed for one's children or for the close animal companions in one's life.

We definitely feel love for cats and, by extension, this

probably tells us something about their capacity to love us back. You do not find people feeling this kind of love, for example, for insects, even though insects fascinate many people. We would find it odd if somebody said they were mad about their praying mantis; in fact, in love with it. That is because we know (or think we know) for certain that a praying mantis cannot love you back.

FIONA KIDMAN

Fred and Daisy and Jodi and Lola

A Personal Narrative

Exits and entrances and all that carry-on. The names of cats I have lived with scroll on like the characters in one of those 1970s movies where couples examine their lives, confess, change places, and are reborn. There is something immensely theatrical about the way cats live, all that sleekness and glamour, the romances and the fighting, the staying out all night, the baring of claws and licking of wounds, the kiss-and-make-up of it all. Only the alcohol and the lipstick are missing. And then, there is the sidling off when the show is over, to the private life.

I hadn't thought much about the private lives of animals until I read a stunning book called *Inside Memory: Pages from a Writer's Workbook*, written by the late Timothy Findley, a Canadian writer and friend. On the cover of the first edition there is a picture of Tiff, as he was known, with one of his eight cats, with its nose touching his chin. (This is, incidentally, the best book I have ever read about the craft and art of writing. I taught it as a set text in my writers' workshops for several years, until my set was gradually 'lost' to writers who clearly loved it as much as I did, and I couldn't replace it.) Tiff wrote a novel based on the lives of the animals on Noah's Ark. He went to live for a time in his dogs' kennels, so that he could research their private habits. What he discovered was astonishing; for instance, the moment of awakening when, he swore, dogs turn to the east, bow to the rising sun and give their morning bark.

But whereas his dogs allowed him to share this intimacy, I don't think cats would. Not only are they private individuals, they possess the sly ability to disappear under scrutiny. I have seen my dog take a crap many times; I've only seen a cat at it once or twice. Cats make a lot of noise when they have sex (from a human perspective you could hardly call this rapacious mauling of females an act of love), but generally they keep it out of sight. And cats, if they can, will take themselves away to die. In the end, their suffering is their own affair. That's not to say I have never witnessed the death of a cat: we lost one in childbirth, another adolescent died of a worm so large it was nearly as big as the kitten itself (this was a long time ago, I am sure he could have been cured now), we have suffered hit-and-run accidents and other violent acts, and I have said fraught and tearful goodbyes to the frail elderly for whom euthanasia was an option. Those are absolutely the worst. We have also parted, once and only once, with a cat we couldn't live with. This cat was intent on smothering one of our children in their cot. Never mind; he got to live with my father instead, and enjoyed a royal and cosseted old age.

My father had a passion for cats. He was chronically hard up, but he always had nice clothes and good cats. The only public office he ever held was as President of the Rotorua Cat Society, some time in the 1960s, chairing a group of cat fanciers who placed their animals on display once a year. But a contradiction presented itself from the outset. There is a difference between exhibiting animals, particularly cats, and being concerned about their welfare, which was really what interested my father. If cats present themselves in a theatrical manner, it is on their terms, not that of humans. Perhaps some are born and bred to showbiz but, on the whole, they would prefer to be left curled up in the sun, or out stalking a mouse — or butterflies, in the case of Lola, the cat who lives with us now. They put themselves on display when they want warmth or food, then they become dynamos of charm. Otherwise, a caged cat is at best forbearing, at worst a sullen beast.

I think my father knew that, for his presidency lasted just a year, and didn't end happily. A large and gloomy room was hired for the Cat Show, scheduled to take place one Saturday afternoon. The Mayor was busy, but the Mayoress agreed to open the show. My father prepared a speech that he rehearsed many times, for he had a perpetual stammer and had never made a speech before. I loved his bravery and the effort that this anticipated appearance cost him.

On Show Day my mother and I appeared to give support, dressed with a certain formality, as befitting the family of the President. Time passed slowly that long afternoon. The cats sat round sulking in their little pens while children poked their fingers through the bars, and wept when they were scratched. Some perfectly ordinary-looking moggies turned nasty. The Mayoress didn't show, and my father walked around the stage (yes, the room was sometimes used as a theatre), smoking several cigarettes, looking lost.

Finally she turned up, wearing a floral dress, a pillbox, white gloves and her bag slung from her wrist. It was four o'clock in the afternoon, and most of the fanciers had left. The Mayoress thought she had come for a flower show; my father thanked her for coming, but forgot to shake hands, and passed on his speech. After that, we got on the bus and went home.

You may notice that there is no mention of my father having had a cat in the show. He had decided it would all be too much of an ordeal for his and my mother's elderly tom. He didn't go back to the Cat Society. Along the way, I think he realised that exhibiting cats was as contrary to nature as was his own shy appearance in public.

Where my father and I disagreed over cats was in his view that they owed a debt of affection to those who lavished care on them. He would worry and fret over a cat who was lacking in this respect. It's not an affectionate cat, he would grumble. Whereas I have always known that a cat belongs only to itself.

Although my mother liked cats too, it was largely due to my father that I always have a cat wherever we live. There are only those anguished days between the death of one cat and the arrival of another that have been empty of their presence. When I sat down to write this, I tried to think of a cat that stood out for me, who radiated a sense of being special over the others. But the room filled with the presence of several (never mind Lola, the white cat who is asleep on the warm part of my computer as I write). She is a long-term guest in the house. Like her, not all of the cats have been mine. Although who can truly claim to possess a cat?

They are self-possessed creatures in a way that humans rarely are. But they seem also to reflect a microcosm of human foible that makes me think about character when I write.

I don't want to infer that cats have human personalities. I've never been particularly interested in anthropomorphism, once I got past *Winnie the Pooh* — and that story is really about a boy learning the harsh reality that grown-up life does not always accommodate the imagination. And I detested the musical *Cats*, which seemed foolishly pretentious. Why would anyone try to be a cat? We can learn from their grace, perhaps, but we cannot be cats, any more that they can write a sonnet or sing opera.

If any cat presented himself as a character ready-made, it was a black Persian who walked in off the street and into my husband's office at the school where he worked, took a lift home and found his way into one of my books. He made a stylish entrance; he was young, dashing and cheerful, like an educational-book rep, although it was soon clear that he had only himself and his charm to offer. He looked for a saucer of milk and, when his needs were met, settled in with the languid assumption that he was there to stay. After a few days of hunting for his owner, it was clear that he was homeless, and his after-hours presence in the school had to stop. He was shown the door. That afternoon, when it came time for Ian to go home, the cat was waiting for the car door to be opened. He sailed home, purring all the way. It's a myth, by the way, that cats don't like cars. Some of them don't, but others regard them as a special treat. For a long time we drove a Siamese cat called Oscar around in our Fiat 600; he enjoyed Sunday drives as much as we did, and was partial to beaches and the fag ends of ice creams.

Fred, as we called the black cat, settled in, and soon I was his favourite person, even if I hadn't engineered his arrival. I have never had a Latin lover, but if I had, I think he'd have been like Fred: sleek, sinuous, gently insistent in his attentions, given to violent passion. In my novel *The Book of Secrets* there are two witch characters, a woman and her granddaughter, caught up in the migrations of a group of Highlanders who come to New Zealand in the 1850s, via a long sojourn in Nova Scotia. The older woman, Isabella, spends a day on her own, grieving over the death of a friend:

> She leaned and stroked her cat, Noah. She did not know where he had come from. One day he had simply appeared at her door, sleek and rather overfed. Yet nobody had laid claim to him and so he had come to live with her. He had wide eyes like a slice of the moon, and his coat was long and black and fluffy. Under his chin there was a bib of white which gave him a slightly petulant air, as if his lip was drooping. He loved Isabella with a passion which she might have found embarrassing had he been human.

So, as Isabella stretches herself in the Nova Scotian sun and reflects, Noah leaps up beside her,

> . . . nuzzling under her armpits, driven wild by the accumulated sweat in the matted cloth of her winter garments. He nibbled fiercely as if he were having a meal, then folded his body down the length of hers, purring a loud noisy dribbling purr until he slept so deeply that they both entered a long period of stillness.

The sun drops away. Noah stirs and minces down the path, looking for a bird. Isabella feels guilt for her wasted day, when suddenly Noah turns his attention on her again.

> In the garden she heard his high piping miaow, a kind of *nya, nya, nya* in the back of his throat as he flung himself at her. He landed on her back, digging in all his claws, seemingly determined to injure her yet loving her as well as he kneaded his paws backwards and forwards in her flesh, only a stray claw reminding her that he was not to be trusted.

While I plead innocent of matted clothes, I know nothing turns a cat on like a well-worn winter jersey. And yes, I identify with Isabella, and Noah is Fred and I think of myself as having been in love with Fred, more than simply loving him. He represents all that engrossing physical pleasure that cats bring, the animal warmth that is different from other contacts of the flesh. The sort of warmth that stops lonely people from going crazy and keeps just ordinary people contented. Because cats don't stay connected with you if you don't stay still, and let them do their work on you. There is a discipline required if one is to be loved by a cat.

Fred's exit was Shakespearian in its tragedy. A dog came as a temporary visitor to our house. The first night he was with us, he chased Fred up the floor-to-ceiling green velvet curtains we had in our bedroom at that time, snapping hard at his heels. We hauled down a distraught Fred. He seemed put out but unhurt, although there seemed to me a paleness about his nose. He took himself off for some fresh air. Time passed: I tried to persuade myself that I had imagined his appearance of being unwell. We never saw him again. Well, not alive. Weeks later, the dog appeared, wearing a ruff of dried black fur round his neck.

Fred's place was taken by Daisy, who was jet black with great golden eyes from which she took her name. She was tiny and short haired. When I look back, Daisy was the only cat I have ever chosen myself. After Fred's death was established, we took ourselves off to the SPCA to find a replacement. Ian fancied a grey cat with a pink nose. I never cared much for pink-nosed cats (present company excluded), but seeing how taken he was, I said nothing. The cat returned his interest with a fiery display of temper and a deep scratch.

I looked up to a cage high in the room and there was Daisy, sweet, peaceful, ready to be taken home. I entered then into a friendship which lasted for more than a dozen years. She was never robust, but she had the kindest, most unassuming temperament of any cat I have ever known. Daisy returned affection, not dutifully, but in a way that suggested our relationship was mutual. She was a tolerant cat. She suffered our absences and rewarded our returns with an enthusiasm that made it worth coming home just to see her. In a lovely poem called 'Cat in an Empty Apartment', the Polish writer Wislawa Symborska, writes:

. . . what can a cat do
in an empty apartment?
Climb the walls?
Rub up against the furniture?
Nothing seems different here,
But nothing is the same.

Something in this poem reminds me of Daisy, how she might have felt when we were not around. As a character, she appears in the guise of loyal friend, there when needed, affectionate, undemanding, uncritical except for a few likes and dislikes in the food department.

By the time that Daisy hovered into invalidism, another cat had joined us in the house. My mother came to live with us and brought Jane with her. I wish I could have liked Jane better; it was war from the beginning. She was a heavy ginger, white and black animal who ruled all our lives, my mother's included. Jane slept on her bed and demanded at least half of it, refused to toilet outside, drew blood if she was crossed, and was intent on making Daisy's life miserable, even though she was the resident cat. Jane was a Top Cat.

Jane and Daisy's fraught relationship continued for a couple of years, reminding me of two aunts of mine who lived together for twenty years, often not exchanging as many words in a day; words that had to be spoken, but nothing more. I loved both of these doting aunts, but it was hard to believe sometimes that they were sisters. One of them was elegant, invalid-ish, and given to telling people that her sister's house was hers. The other was energetic, sociable in a more boisterous sense, and black and white in her views. Daisy, to some extent, and Jane. Both cats limped into old age at roughly the same time, perhaps worn out by their bickering. We parted with Daisy when she could no longer stand to eat her meals; Jane left us one morning in my mother's arms. My mother thought Jane would lie there and go into a gentle sleep, but death by injection is not like that. They don't tell us, from their death chambers in Texas, that death is almost but not quite as fast as the needle; there is the moment of blind panic as the lethal liquid reaches the heart, the last defiant snarl.

By then our house had become a permanent guest-house for colourful characters. Our granddaughter came to stay for a while and brought Jodi with her, a grey cat with a large white bib that ages her appearance. She looks as old men do with napkins tied under their chins. The house was pretty well full by then, so Jodi, already middle-aged, settled comfortably into the garden shed at the end of our lawn. That was seven years ago, and Jodi has come and gone more times than I can recall, as her owner has moved house. Jodi is living with us right now, but soon she will board a plane and fly to Dunedin. In the early days of her peripatetic life, Jodi went missing several times, causing us heartbreak and despair at the thought of never seeing her again.

My mother went to live at the Home of Compassion at Island Bay in Wellington. She was rediscovering her staunch Presbyterian beginnings, yet seemed curiously happy to be amongst those whom my bossy aunt would have described as heathens. Indeed, her best friend, acquired when she was in her mid-eighties, was a nun who lived in the room next door. My mother maintained rational conversations until the day she died — her last advice to me was to make sure I didn't leave my clothes dryer on at nights, as this was the most common cause of house fires, and she had noticed that I did this rather a lot.

All the same, she did have a period of some six weeks in which she 'saw' things we could not. She looked out onto the golf course, beyond the beautiful garden frieze outside her window, and saw men making hay. Other days she saw sheep. In the evenings, she called for sherry parties with the nurses and directed them along unseen verandahs to find something to eat, or out to the tennis court for a quick game — as if she was living the last bit of glamour that she and her sisters had enjoyed in their youth on a long-lost sheep station. And it was during this period that Jodi went missing from a Newtown house.

Her owner had called her night and day for six weeks and we all knew, I mean *knew* that Jodi had gone. But not my mother. She was a protective spirit and a guiding light in our family and was upset to see her great-granddaughter so upset. The cat was not missing, she insisted. In fact, she could see the cat. It was outside under a camellia tree; it had walked up the corridor and into her room the night before; no, she didn't know how it had walked such a distance, perhaps it had got on the bumper of someone's car and ridden there, but she was there and if we just looked we would see her. We nodded patiently, sighed and continued our night vigils in a bleak Newtown street, calling for Jodi. Sometimes I believed I could see her shape in a tree, something would flicker in nearby grass, but it was just shadows in a wind-blown night.

One afternoon the cat reappeared — thin, tired, but still herself — at my granddaughter's door. There, my mother said, when she heard the news, the day before the lecture on the clothes dryer, I told you she was there. Shortly afterwards, she died.

Jodi disappeared for about the same length of time after another shift. When she turned up again, it was agreed that whenever her other living arrangements might seem temporary or unsatisfactory, she would move back to our garden shed. This suits her fine. She has become amiable, contented and matronly. I see something of myself in her, a restless spirit who sometimes seemed more away from home than I really was; now, like Jodi, I am happy to stay at home, satisfied with the sense of continuity that it brings.

Which brings me to Lola, the blonde amputee star who lives with us too, because her owner lives in an apartment that doesn't take cats. She is snow white and deaf, has one bright-green eye and one a slightly watery blue, and half a tail. She is an amputee on account of her deafness; because she can't hear, she didn't move out of the path of an oncoming car. There are more ways of killing a cat than choking her with cream, as Rudyard Kipling once famously said.

Lola reminds me of Marilyn Monroe. I have a large black-and-white portrait of Monroe, photographed at Malibu in 1962, in the room where I work. She is holding a slipper of champagne and leans on a balcony railing overlooking a valley. She has that cloud of white-blonde hair for which she was famous, and she is exposing her gums as she smiles, something I've always suspected men find attractive, as if the mouth is totally open and receptive. You could say she looks brimming with life, but if you look more closely, you will see the beginning of middle age around the chin and throat. If you didn't know who it was and she was wearing a scarf over her hair, you might think that here was a moderately pretty woman wearing the stain of pain.

Lola is like that. She has suffered the loss of a part of herself, as well as the loss of her brother Claude who lived with her for the first year or so of her life. She may be short-sighted as well, for she is forever chasing shadows. A glass or a ring that catches sunlight will drive her to distraction. To make up for it all she practises pretty, with an exhibitionist's flair. Green and white is my favourite colour combination, and it seems as if she must know this, for she is constantly arranging and rearranging herself on my sea-green cushions, her brilliant white coat showing up my beggared sofa as rather off-white. She smooches the white roses and drapes herself over the jasmine trellis, constantly colour-coordinating herself. She is a cat that makes us call to each other over and again, come and look. Just look what that cat is doing now. How cute she is as she rolls and stretches and catches a piece of our clothing with her claw. How infuriating she is, as she minces along a desk in our bedroom where we keep bric-a-brac from our travels, curling her paw around objects and sending them flying. *Time for breakfast.* Smash goes the delicate Vietnamese vase. *Get up, will you.* Crash goes that piece of expensive Murano glass, bought in a moment of madness. *Pay attention.* Goodbye to that little Limoges dish of my mother's that I keep for sentimental reasons. The hedonist at work.

So here she is, right now, confronting me with twitching white stump, from the top of the computer. The light shines through her pink ears. She yawns in my face, her mouth like a pale peony unfolding. Those pink gums. This is the signal that its time for me to stop work and feed my film-star guest. And I'll do that, because for the moment Jodi is still living her patient elderly life in the garden shed, and she will be a target for the leading lady's wrath if I don't perform.

These cats have wriggled their way into my heart, and some day I know they will have to take their leave, one on a plane to hundreds of miles away, the other to a house with a garden, returning to their real homes. Then I fear the business of falling in love will have to begin all over again.

What I don't know is whether they will remember us, when they have gone, in the way I remember them. Dogs pine away and die in the absence of their owners, but I don't think cats do. They are just happier when the right person turns up. Later, Symborska's poem goes on:

Footsteps on the staircase,
But they're new ones.
The hand that puts fish on the saucer
Has changed too.

Something doesn't start
At its usual time.
Something doesn't happen as it should.
Someone was always, always here,
Then suddenly disappeared
And stubbornly stay disappeared.

You can't do that to a cat. When Jodi used to go missing, we called at the very same spot as she was found, over and over again, night after night, bringing offerings, delicacies, fish, fresh chicken. We believed she watched us. But in the end, the only person she allowed to scoop her up off the dark streets was the person to whom she truly belongs. Or, perhaps, belongs to her. If we do not possess our cats, in the end, we may be possessed by them.

More than we will ever know.

DOUGLAS WRIGHT

The Human Miaow

When I see a cat drenched to the bone it shocks me into laughter. And then silence. All their character seems stripped away, they appear to be less than half their normal size, totems of misery, crying.

It reminds me that each hair of their fur coat is a vital living thing with its own story of being licked, petted, bitten, scratched, looked at, baked in the sun. Once dry they wrap themselves inside these stories and take their rightful place in our lives.

But they don't really need us. Cats know how to be alone. They are self-contained. This hermetic quality make their gifts of attention to humans something specially granted, seductive. Perhaps that's why we once worshipped them and had them placed, mummified, in our tombs so they could watch over us on our journey to the Land of the Dead. My own cat, Alice Thumb, can be severe in her aloofness; strategic. Sometimes she will ignore me all day then I'll feel her gaze, tactile as fur, and see in her pinwheeling golden eyes the lost pride, the mother-of-cats, the orphaned litter. Her eyes caress me as if I'm one vast nipple she can suck on forever. And at night, in bed, she presses the length of her tortoiseshell body against mine, purring ferociously, dribbling and kneading with her claws in the place where she deems this imaginary nipple to be.

Its exact position has never been made clear; it keeps shifting, like a beauty spot in Proust.

She is a keen hunter, bringing me severed lizards, silenced cicadas and once a giant moth with grass-green wings whose soft twiggy body was covered in a beard of moss. It was still alive, its wings ragged, and I thanked her before letting it go. She is partial to such rituals.

Alice has a talent for sleeping, curling herself up into a mollusc of fur, dreaming no doubt of other nests.

But do cats dream?

Sometimes I think my whole reality is dreamed by my cat.

For those of us who live alone, a cat can take the place of an entire family. Threads of dreaming (if we allow dreaming), the habitual feeding, stroking, talking develop into a private language akin to that of lovers or Siamese twins. This language is different with each cat, and when the long-loved pet dies and takes up its place just outside the corners of our eyes it's often the special call, the human miaow, that is the last vestige of its presence. Let it out accidentally on your new cat and it is like calling a new lover by your old lover's name. It just slips out.

Istina!

Leo!

Alice Thumb?

So this language develops over years and it is a secret language, sometimes even from those who speak it. It's also something, perhaps, to be ashamed of, as is our extreme grief at the death of the beloved animal. That is private, hidden.

My cat teaches me. She moves without premeditation, as

if the movement itself were the thought and no watching eyes could rob it of its spontaneity.

Once when she brought inside a bird that was still alive, its wings flapping red, I didn't know whether to make her let it go or to sink my teeth into its throat to help her kill it. Her ferocity revives something native in me.

When Alice herds me by figure-eighting between and around my legs, I know she's persuading me to the fridge, where her meat lives, so to speak. But I don't think she's cunning or greedy. I feel as if we're dancing the infinity symbol together and that our wills, rather than being opposed, are being plaited by some third force which basks in our symbiosis.

Like humans, providing they haven't been wounded beyond repair, cats love to be stroked. To touch and be touched by them can feed a deep hunger.

Once a friend of mine, a recluse whose cat had just been 'put down', told me that the cat itself had asked her to let it die. I think sometimes we treat animals rather more humanely than we do our fellow humans, who must be made to live until their last natural breath, prolonged as long as possible.

Big cats were once our predators and we huddled around fires in fear of their sabre-tooth fangs and rabid claws. I once had a dream in which I was lying in a half-darkened room. At first I thought I was alone. Then I noticed a giant cat, a golden lion with eyes glowing like embers in the dark, lying on the other side of the small room. It was completely still, apart from the cage of its breathing, and exuded an invitation to caress it, to join it. But in the dream I was seized with a profound fear; my blood froze. For some dream reason I had some small pieces of meat with me and in desperation I chewed them until they were tender and then spat them in a path leading away from me so the big cat would leave me alone. I was so terrified I would probably have bitten off parts of my own body if I'd had to. And, eventually, it went, with a lingering farewell gaze. I still regret not going with it.

BERYL FLETCHER

Cat as Memoir

A woman and a boy and a cat are hiding in a hut near a remote West Coast beach. The woman has not been here before. The cat is tiny, her name is Black. She is slung in a cotton baby carrier because she is too small to run through the thick bush. She is a gift from the boy to the woman, for her friendship, her support of him when he cries in the night, for the unlimited and safe access to her body wherever and whenever he wants.

They are hiding inside a hut that the boy built for himself two years before, when he was just sixteen. He has brought her here to show her his teenage fantasy, a place of refuge for him and his mates if some bastard, dunno who, decided to blast the North Island into an atomic ground zero. The hut is solidly built with a corrugated-iron roof and four wooden bunks. On one side is a brick chimney and an open fireplace, an iron pot, grey ashes, and lumps of blackened charcoal. The woman is impressed with the hut. She had expected a primitive lean-to inhabited by possums and rats but this is a true refuge. And today it has become just that, not from bombs, but from bogans.

An hour before, they had climbed the steep hill through the thick undergrowth of regenerating bush, up to where the trees are tall and old and riven with low-riding kereru that startle the woman with their sudden wings. They come to a small cleared space in front of the hut and stop to smoke another joint and watch flocks of painted butterflies drink moisture from their bare legs. No wind, not a breath. It is Black who alerts them, bolt upright in her carry-sack, ears quivering. She can hear something or somebody says the boy, and from the look of her body, it ain't good. The woman, unused to smoking flower-heads of such purity, hears nothing except the music playing in her head. They go into the hut and the boy padlocks the door from the inside. He blows some smoke from the end of the joint into the cat's mouth to keep her quiet.

The woman peers through a gap in the wall and sees three men creeping through the bush carrying crossbows. They look mean and rough and she is afraid. One of them tries to open the door. After a few minutes, they move off without speaking. That's what frightens her the most: their absolute silence.

They wait for a while, then the boy whispers, we're outa here. They begin the long trek back to the road, making as little noise as possible. All at once an arrow hits the trunk of a tree just above the woman's head. The speed of it, the depth of the penetration into the trunk of the puriri, shocks her. Her legs turn to jelly. Shit, says the boy, they are hunting us for real, keep as quiet as you can.

For the next hour, the two sides play a deadly game of hide and seek. Towards the end, the hunted ones take refuge high up in a tree. It is easy to climb this particular tree because the boy in his ground zero days had taken the precaution of nailing bits of plank to the trunk and covering them with bark to provide camouflage. This formed a crude ladder. There is a small platform at the top of the ladder and a wooden box containing glass bottles of water and tins of sardines and baked beans. The boy says there is enough here for us to survive for days.

The woman is fearful of being trapped up here but the boy says just watch the cat, Black will tell us when they are nearby. And it's true, she does. Her fur spikes up and her ears tremble a good minute before one of the hunters comes into view and leans against the trunk of their tree and rolls himself a smoke. He has a mullet haircut and grimy fingers. Black is motionless, still as the air. Eventually, the bogan lifts his bow and disappears into the bush. That's the last they see of him or the other two. Black yawns and drifts into a deep sleep. The woman and the boy climb down the tree and make their way to the road. That night, the boy tells everyone back at the farm that Black was better than any dog at sensing danger.

That was the end of it. Well, not quite. Afterwards, the woman wondered if she had dreamt the whole thing or if the bogan who had shot an arrow at her had mistaken her for a deer; that's until she found out that there were no deer in that particular part of the bush and no wild pigs either. How do I know this? I was that woman and this story belongs to me. It's true, every word of it, or, to be honest, as much as I choose to remember (or reveal) about it from the distance of twenty-nine years.

Black taught me many lessons, the most valuable being that cats may appear to be bending to their owners' will but they never do. Black was a vegetarian cat, she was raised on vegetable purée and crushed soy beans. One night, coming home down the long drive to the old farmhouse where I lived communally with nine others, I saw two cats creeping along in the long grass next to the driveway. I stopped the car. It was

Black, accompanied by a feral cat, a great scarred ginger hoon who lived in the hay barn. I watched these two cats for over half an hour and I was astounded to see the feral cat teaching my pampered vegetarian how to catch and devour rabbits. Cats are not meant to be able to hunt co-operatively but these two did. Maybe they hadn't read the same textbook on animal behaviour that I had. From that day on, I fed Black real cat food like murdered horses and fish heads out of tins. Anything rather than a repeat performance from the bedraggled creature with bloodied paws and a huge extended stomach that tried to get under the covers with me that night.

Black became a travelling cat. She loved the bush and the sea and unlike any cat I have owned, she did not seem to require a stable place to live in to be contented. Just like me at the time. I drove that cat all over the North Island; she slept in cabins and tents and on the bush floor, in rain and sun and wind. I was in my mid-thirties at the time and a born-again hippy, recently set free from a disastrous marriage, free to revel in the sexual and cultural revolution of 1970s New Zealand.

Eventually, I left both the boy and the cat to have further adventures. But I never forgot Black and the uncanny fact that this cat was just as restless as I was at that particular stage of my life. She was never more content than when she was on the move, travelling light, always in the process of going somewhere else.

Gore Vidal once said that memoir has nothing to do with history, it's *how one remembers one's life*. Of the many definitions and analyses that attempt to explain the essence/structure of memoir, Vidal's is my favourite. On the one hand, we have the fluidity and irrationality of memory, irrational in the sense that it is often the most seemingly trivial events that come back to haunt us. On the other hand, we have this urge to make a logical and thematically relevant narrative of our own experience. This is the *how* in Vidal's definition. It has become my habit to use the personalities of my cats to make thematic sense of both my past and my present. My *how* is a cat.

How could it be anything else? Each cat that I have owned (thirteen in number) seems to reflect the essential aspects of my life during the time of our mutual ownership. Take the above-mentioned Black, the hippy traveller. Take Tosca, the caterwauling coloratura, given to singing feline versions of Puccini arias from the top of a phoenix palm in my early days in Auckland when I was studying opera. Take Mercy, my tabby kitten who became a snake-killer at the age of six months when I lived on a bush property in New South Wales. Mercy taught me about the bravery of cats when she confronted a deadly red-bellied snake that had decided to come to my back door in search of water during a long drought. Mercy killed three more snakes that week before she became flushed with success and momentarily dropped her guard. Watching from the kitchen window, I learned how quickly a cat can die when a poisonous snake makes a fatal strike at its neck. (Twenty-five seconds, if you must know.) And later, I learned from an old bush-hand never to leave water or milk outside for my cats because this brought the snakes close to the house.

My hippy days of sex and drugs and rock and roll are long gone. Now that I am a writer, I live more vicariously, one step removed from real, lived experience. I am irretrievably in love with mobile phones, digital TV, DVDs, and that most brilliant of inventions, the Internet. I am bored witless with dead-end philosophic arguments about the tension between the virtual and the real. My current cat Hecate has never had to work this out, she already knows the answer. The real is the real is the real. This cat, a rescued stray of devastating intelligence, is an ideal writer's cat because she provides an antidote to the necessary 'away with the birdies' state that writers enter day after day in order to produce their work. She grounds me, brings me back to the truly essential facts of life. She knows every nook and cranny in the house and garden, every dust ball, every leaf and plant; she knows the best place to find a rat or a mouse or a rabbit; she knows the best position on the deck to torment the piwakawaka feeding high up in the mamaku tree-fern. If the slightest change occurs, she checks it out. If I tidy a cupboard (a rare event given the above-mentioned 'away with the birdies' phenomenon), she gets into the cupboard afterwards to make sure that all is present and correct. If I move anything or bring something new into the house, she creates a scene. When visitors arrive, she provides an elaborate and rather embarrassing security check by sniffing the visitors' feet, then sitting on their shoes until they are ready to depart. When I get too far into abstract territory, she reminds me about the true meaning of life (kill or be killed) by bringing me gifts of half-eaten mice, live rabbits, bird feathers, or chewed KFC bones stolen from the rubbish bin up on the road.

I revere cats because they are able to attach themselves passionately to a particular place, an enviable state of being that, no matter how hard I try, I have never been able to emulate. Cats own the environment in a minute fashion, they know their landscape, both geographical and emotional, and everything that moves, breathes or changes within it.

Hecate takes this special ability of cats to a level I have never witnessed in any of my prior felines and this is one reason out of many that makes her so special to me. I have always found it difficult to become emotionally attached to houses or land or possessions, and when I see Hecate reigning so successfully over her little queendom, I bow to her superior wisdom.

She knows something I don't, and if she deigns to stay with me for a few more years, maybe I'll learn it too.

BRIAN TURNER

Extract from 'Cats and Dogs'

My neighbours own cats. Annette has one called Boots. She is black with a white belly, white paws, and is sleek. I like the way she prowls around my section, checking out the territory. On one of Annette's doors is a sign, 'Dogs have Masters, Cats have Servants'. It's impossible to disagree. Boots is all the things I associate with cats: imperious, mostly indifferent, callous with mice and birds and rabbits, uncooperative, and unhurried, except when threatened. Boots is okay; she deigns to allow me to pat her, now and then, and is unashamedly solicitous, especially when she wants food. She sips water with the priggish air of a Minister of Finance weary of listening to carpers.

Sue and Pete's cat, Willie Kirk, is a neutered ginger tom. He is burly, and a noted nosy parker. He sits and watches the world go by. I am sure Willie sneers at me. Willie brings rabbits into the house; he will steal a trout from Pete's bag given the chance. He watches TV — *The Simpsons* and *Country Calendar*. He used to be intrigued by the dog show. He is famous. The local vet, for instance, addressed his account to Willie Kirk, Main Road, Oturehua.

Sue has a photo album devoted solely to The Life and Times of Willie Kirk. There are photos of Willie emerging after having, unintentionally, done several rounds in a clothes dryer.

There is Willie chasing and retrieving bottle tops; Willie riding in a wheelbarrow, and another of him surrounded by a ripped-up roll of paper towels. 'He does that,' says Sue, 'when he fails to get his own way.' She says he is her 'surrogate grandchild'.

And Pete proudly says, 'Willie is highly intelligent, and a magnificent hunter.'

I suspect Willie thinks I am silly. Why? Because I shout at the TV when I am watching rugby, turn off *Holmes* the minute he starts to orchestrate another bout of national grieving, and because, the other day, I thought he looked so richly resplendent sitting on a fence post in the moonlight that I 'looked up to the stars above' and sang, 'O lovely Pussy! O Pussy, my love, / What a beautiful Pussy you are!'

But, as all who observe animals know — Willie excepted perhaps — it is impossible to amuse a cat. Disdain is their peerless art, gratitude a quality denied them.

Dogs are different; anyone can make them wag their tails, retrieve a ball or a stick, and express panting, undying devotion. But in all my years of cat-watching, I've never seen one grin, like the Cheshire in *Alice In Wonderland*, for even so much as a second.

Women generally seem to like cats, who slink rather than stink, more than men like them. Maybe it's because women are so good at being nasty while appearing innocuous, just as men are masterly at being brutal while seeming to be rational, which may be why men, and tomboys, seem to prefer dogs, and women, overwhelmingly, go for cats. (I know, I know, there will be a great many exceptions to this, and that some of you will be called Marmaduke and Fiona.)

Recently, apropos of women's propensities, I liked reading

the opinion of *Otago Daily Times* columnist 'Civis' that, 'Womanhood is a kind of freemasonry bound by the scent of flowers.' I nodded, and then thought I'd like to add, 'and cats'.

I've lost count of the number of times women have told me that men don't understand cats. That's true of me, I reply, and add that I understand hardly anything, although I am interested in a great deal which, possibly, is why I am confused so much of the time. Unlike me, cats seldom appear confused, and yet some cats — and dogs, for that matter — chase their tails occasionally. And both can kick up a fuss. In his 'Song of Myself' Walt Whitman was wrong to say, of animals in general, that: 'they are so placid and self-contain'd', and, 'They do not sweat and whine about their condition'.

While I'm not one to knock the great Walt, for him to talk of thinking of turning 'to live with animals' was ridiculous. Animals would tear most of us apart. I'd sooner put up with people discussing their duty to God than have to try to avoid a big cat interested only in filling its belly with bits of bloodied me. Walt was right to be contemptuous of humans and their 'demented . . . mania of owning things' but I'd still prefer most people to the company of a collateral of hungry cats and dogs.

As for stern old T. S. Eliot and his liking for cats, meow, his favourite 'Morgan' may, harmlessly, have liked his 'Devonshire cream in a bowl', but he was also, darling creature, 'partial to partridges, likewise to grouse'. Me too, actually.

As for gingery Willie of Oturehua, he eats anything, which is a problem. Pete says that, recently, 'he hoed into the leg of a Hereford that I brought home for the dogs, and he's been farting so much that we won't let him on the couch in the lounge.'

I have concluded that there'll never be another quite like Willie.

PETER WELLS

On Attending the Death of a Cat

For Gwendolyn

There's a curious pain in attending a pet's death. My mother has told me that a friend of hers, a woman in her eighties, wept for her cat's death in a bereft way she'd never wept when her husband died. There's a pathos in a pet dying. One is, through one's god-like agency, more implicated. Whether it's done unseen or you're holding the animal in your arms, as I was when my lovely old cat of seventeen years underwent a consciousness that something untoward was happening — followed by that abrupt slumping down, equivalent of the last breath — you're still implicated.

Some little voice whispers: you killed the cat. You killed the object of all your affections. This largely silent, unspeaking animal, who has given you its attention, affection, its loyalty — who has played a part in your life, often more constant than a lover — has been 'put out of its misery' by you — the person who claims to love it the most.

All those phrases we exchange between people who have animals: 'It was for the best'. 'You did the kindest thing'. 'She had a good life.' We say these things, hoping against hope they'll allay the pain. But they don't. They can't. There's always a hidden little rip of savagery inside your human breast: and it is as if in the prism of a pet's life, you feel all the torments of human separations, infidelities and losses. I say infidelity, because in some senses death is the ultimate infidelity. One is abandoned, left behind. The dead body voyages on. Into nothingness perhaps, into non-existence. It is we who are left behind: the bereaved.

There is nothing more laughable than the emotion spent on the death of pets. There is nothing as painful as the death of your own pet. This is the conundrum.

It sometimes amazes me, the twin poles involved in the love of a cat. There is, on one hand, the embarrassing excess of emotions which calcify into cuteness. I'm no exception to the rule. If the world knew the private language I pour into my cat's ear, I would feel exposed.

But there's also something profound which a pet can bring to the surface. Submerged feelings of love, but also deeper feelings to do with protection, nurture and obligation. It is good to be needed. Probably all of us as humans wrestle with the sense of the meaninglessness of our existence: who would care, ultimately, if we lived or died. A pet would. A pet needs to be fed, and let outside, and then let inside. The letting inside is what is important. One allows a dumb animal (dumb in the sense of silent, lacking speech) access to so many feelings one wouldn't dream of telling another person. Hurt, loss, pain, grief, disappointment. And that most difficult, baffling thing of all, which causes so much mayhem — love.

This love is a very straightforward thing — seldom betrayed — until death. As I said earlier, death is a form of betrayal: the cat goes on into an afterworld or does not, depending on your beliefs — but we are left behind. Until we get our next cat.

I'm no exception to the rule here. After my last cat died — to use pet-parlance, was 'put down' — I decided I would live for a while without a cat. But within eighteen months a stray had found my door. I could not turn her away. Enter: a 'new' cat.

When a pet dies, a lot goes with it — the accompanying blur of time. It's not as if only the pet dies, but it's as if the cat acts as a prompt to all sorts of memory — who found the animal; how obligations may have passed on from one member of the family (younger) to another (older); how an animal is domesticated; how an animal retains some element of wildness; the unknowableness of an animal; the silent loyalty of an animal. Yes, it is the silent loyalty which is most telling. Is there any more poignant expression of grief, and loyalty, than the animal — a dog in this case — which appeared at the Japanese train station, to await its master? For years and years. Of course it is dumb, in a profound sense. It is both stupid literally — everyone with any sense knows the master will never return — and it's dumb in a more mystical sense, as in dumb show: there's something plangent which speaks straight to the heart here. In some senses we are all that dog which turns up to the train expecting someone to get off: in this single act we see a metaphor for grief, and memory — and love.

So the killing of a pet, to be brutal, is a most difficult act: it requires the kind of philosophical weighing which lies behind the act of euthanasia: the rational perception of the pain of the animal is weighed against the emotional distress involved in participating in the animal's demise. This is where those cute little phrases come in — phrases almost suitable for a Hallmark card — phrases which betray our uneasiness. It was for the best . . . he had a good innings . . . better for him . . .

No matter how we dress up these statements, behind them screams a single sentence: I killed the cat! In a very ordinary way I took part in an execution. I ordered the execution. And it is then we look beneath the surface — the avoidance of mess; the inability, in a suburban or urban setting, for us to put up with faeces, blood and gore. The unpleasantness of witnessing an animal's decrepitude, in which we may see, only too clearly, a forewarning of our own. In arranging the killing, we also establish the obscured nature of power in the owner–pet relationship. For many years the fond pet-owner says things like: 'Oh, it's he who runs me.' My mother often said of her cat — something she would never have said of her husband — 'He's the boss!' Spoken wryly, with affection. But come killing-time, it is we who hold the metaphorical gun. And it is we who order the animal to be 'put down'.

Put down where? Do animals have souls? Is there a cosy Catholic kennel in a Michelangelo-decorated heaven? Is there a pretty pet farm in the sky, as Hallmark sentiment dictates? Or do they literally just join with dust, dissolving back to atoms? Pet stories are quite popular, but I don't think I've read many about an animal's afterlife. It's as if that is stretching the fiction of a pet's anima too far. A pet is of this world. A pet is of this life. A pet is like a watermelon warm in the sun, or a piece of fruit hanging ripe on the tree. That's its high point, its essence, the rationale for its being. At least in our cosmos — the world of the human.

Yet I suppose the mystery here is why, when we can kill our pets — when we can philosophically and psychologically accept that it is, on reflection, the better of two equations (live and suffer, die and end suffering) — there is so much resistance to euthanasia among humans.

The difference of course in the argument is that pets are beasts and we are humans. Our death means more. To us. As humans. Because it maintains our place in the 'natural order'. But to talk of a natural order in the twenty-first century is a form of black comedy. There is no natural order. Or rather, natural order has become the final refuge of simplistic thinkers like fundamentalists and conservatives. So perhaps, when we go to the killing of our pets, we are also subconsciously preparing ourselves, or obscuring from ourselves, a much bigger equation: how can I agree to kill this animal that I love, yet refrain from offering such mercy to a human that I love? There's a slight act of indecency here, an implausible kindness.

Yet it is necessary. J. M. Coetzee says, 'Animals have only their silence left with which to confront us. Onto this silence we are given the magnificent freedom, the absolute luxury — and folly — to project all our needs.' (Didn't I catch myself just a moment ago murmuring to my new cat, 'That's alright, little one.' Little one. Belittling one.)

I write onto my pet's silence my loneliness, need for love, conversation, company: onto her silence I limn a stalwart watching observing presence. I do not gaze into her eyes wondering what she thinks of me. I accept the little man I am as returned in her serene unblinking stare. But when her eyes become clouded, or her hips refuse to move, I will have to face the difficult task: I will have to make a decision I can't in legal terms make about a human I love as much. This is the conundrum of attending a death of a pet. Wretched, miserable, sick to the soul, yet clamped to the ideal that 'it is necessary' — for the pet and the pet's owner; so the pet, adored, a touchstone for decades, the great soother of heartache, a solitary person's lode of kindness; we must make ourselves stern and expedite the exit: in a reasonless universe, we must act as god. And in this lies perhaps the true pity of being — the owner of a cat.

Until, that is, we meet our next cat.

poems

ELIZABETH SMITHER

A Cat Called Straus

Not the musical family
of Viennese waltzes
but the middle publisher
of Farrar Straus & Giroux.

He will not need to explain
my name has only one 's'
or my ancestors were Jewish cats
or I particularly love books

because all cats are publishers:
every night a new book
arises in the moonlight
over the hunting garden.

Listening to Handel with a Cat

for Bill Sewell

Sometimes — and I think the cat thinks this —
after ordinary, quotidian things

lying stretched on the red tile floor
in the summer heat or reading in a chair

where there is nothing distracting or deep
for Handel seems conservative, even to a cat

music makes its own way, as water does, and swells
with sufficient volume between confining banks

which stalwartly resist — to the exact pitch
of water flow — until, and here the cat

stirs and his whiskers twitch — grandness comes
as if every drop resolves to go, magisterially

and slow and everything is resolve, resolve
and not a drop is wasted, not a vapour

above the darkening river, in the mist
but everything accrues to grand and majestic.

Sleeping Cat

With a paw elevated in air
the cat sleeps. What strange
dynamic allows this?

Is it from his dead-calm spine
such poise arises, like a spring
so loosely coiled, so confident

that a ginger paw can float
as if above a bowl of cream?
The sleeping face seems to grin

at such a thought. Sleep, to cats,
is not the human-tossed thing
but absolute, a King

waking in a blurred circle of courtiers
or a Queen giving birth
before Prime Ministers.

Straus after General Anaesthesia, Dental Extraction and Paw Examination

Eyes dilated so only the merest rim
of yellow outlines the iris. The vet
lifts you out of your top tier cage
and you look like a stuffed animal
no shape in his arms, half-stuffed,
half-china. But in your own cage
after your pain relief is explained
and the fact that you didn't eat all day
you turn suddenly like the segment of a big snake
yearning towards familiar scents and sights.
You like the car going home, you like the cage
and all night, falling off the bed, rolling
on the carpet, eating voraciously from
three bowls: water, jellimeat, Purina
or staggering through the cat flap to walk
a few steps up the path as if someone
watching might see you claiming your territory
you come alive, as much as your black drugged eyes
will allow.

Bernard Brown

Sufficient Pussy

All cats can go to hell
and save me worry.
The only one I ever loved
was one in Auckland
in a curry.

KEVIN IRELAND

King Canary, Queen Cat

The canary was King in the Land
of the Blind Cat. At night he slept safe
in the metal castle of his cage; by day
he swanked around his realm, dodging

the sightless claws that stumbled after
the throat that phrased his regal song.
But sway of eye over ear hangs
on the light, and one evening we forgot

to lock the cage. Later, we could
only too easily imagine how Darkness
must have crouched and listened
as the Kingdom of Appearances dissolved

and cubes of simple optical prediction
warped into a single soundbox of dementia.
Invisible surfaces must have crashed
into his wings, claws pursuing down

a sonic tube, walls melting into echoes —
extensions of the cat's genius.
You said: 'The grisly thought is:
the dark meant *both* of them were blind.'

Then — worse than that —
you asked if I could hear the new anthem
rumbling round the room: Queen Cat
purring on a throne of golden feathers.

James K. Baxter

Tomcat

This tomcat cuts across the
zones of the respectable
through fences, walls, following
other routes, his own. I see
the sad whiskered skull-mouth fall
wide, complainingly, asking

to be picked up and fed, when
I thump up the steps through bush
at 4 p.m. He has no
dignity, thank God! has grown
older, scruffier, the ash-
black coat sporting one or two

flowers like round stars, badges
of bouts and fights. The snake head
is seamed on top with rough scars:
old Samurai! He lodges
in cellars, and the tight furred
scrotum drives him into wars

as if mad, yet tumbling on
the rug looks female, Turkish-
trousered. His bagpipe shriek at
sluggish dawn dragged me out in
pyjamas to comb the bush
(he being under the vet

for septic bites): the old fool
stood, body hard as a board,
heart thudding, hair on end, at
the house corner, terrible,
yelling at something. They said,
'Get him doctored.' I think not.

C. K. Stead

Cat/ullus

Zac's dead
buried with his brother Wallace
beside the carport
under the pongas.

Zac of the goldfish eyes
and nice-smelling fur
who when I had a problem with a poem
slept on it,
who lived to put his paw-print
on a valued citation,
who in his dying days
jumped to swipe at a passing moth
and missed.

Zac the radical,
Zac the bed-crowder
the window leaper
the lateral-thinker,
Zac the head-first rat-eater
is dead,
is 'laid to rest',
has met his match.

Frater, ave (etc)
Black Zac
Zac the Knife.

notes on contributors

James K. Baxter (1926–72), the charismatic and controversial poet, published his first poem when he was eighteen, with over thirty books of poetry published during his lifetime alone, not to mention plays and other writing. Yet he spent much of his time preoccupied with society's outcasts and founding a community for young people amongst the Maori of Jerusalem. He was a man of contradictions: loyal to his country, while frequently condemning its institutions; a devout Roman Catholic, yet leading an unorthodox life. The body of work he left after his early death shows him to be one of the great English-language poets of last century.

Ursula Mary Bethell (1874–1945), was born in Surrey, England. She grew up in New Zealand but was sent to England and to Europe to be educated. After three decades she returned to Christchurch and began to write poetry, where she became a central figure in artistic and cultural life during the thirties. Her first collection of poems, *From a Garden in the Antipodes*, was published in 1929, followed by *Time and Place* (1936) and *Day and Night: Poems 1924–35* (1939).

Peter Bland's memoir, *Sorry, I'm a Stranger Here Myself*, was published in 2004 by Random House. His book of verse for children, *The Night Kite*, was short-listed for the New Zealand Post Children's Book Awards. He is a co-founder of Wellington's Downstage Theatre and a well-known New Zealand poet.

Don't judge **Bernard Brown** by his 'Sufficient Pussy' poem. He was passionately fond of King and Sarah. They bred five long-lived kittens whom Sarah outlasted. She died aged twenty-four and always ate at table. King, ever on the *qui vive*, was run over while pursuing the cause of infidelity. Bernard came via Suffolk and Singapore to New Zealand in 1962 and, apart from four years in New Guinea (and an arrow wound), he has taught law at Auckland University.

Diane Brown's publications include two collections of poetry (*Before the Divorce We Go to Disneyland,* Tandem, 1997 — winner of the NZSA Best First Book of Poetry; *Learning to Lie Together*, Godwit, 2004), two novels (*Eight Stages of Grace* was a finalist in the Montana Book Awards 2003), and a travel memoir (*Liars and Lovers,* Random House, 2004). She is currently writing a novel, *Hooked*, and a prose/poetic work, *Here Comes Another Vital Moment*, and is the co-ordinator and tutor for the Aoraki Polytechnic Advanced Fiction Writing Course in Dunedin.

Janet Charman teaches at an Auckland Secondary School. Her last poetry collection was *Snowing Down South*, published by AUP. Her family's cat is a calico named Girl.

Martin Edmond's *Chronicle of the Unsung* won the biography category at the 2005 Montana Book Awards. His next book, *Luca Antara*, will be published in 2006. He lives in Sydney.

The cats **Barbara Else** has lived with include Nakki, Fatcat, Charlie-cat, Aubrey Strawberry, Enchilada, Alcatraz, Gretel, Orlando, and Stanley the Mad Earl of Derby. She once gave house room to seventeen slightly radioactive Texan salamanders. The latest of Barbara's many novels is *The Case of the Missing Kitchen*. She has edited various story collections, most recently *Mischief and Mayhem* for children, and *Like Wallpaper* for teenagers (both Random House, 2005). She has been Writing Fellow at Victoria University, was awarded a CNZ Scholarship in Letters and in 2005 was made a Member of the New Zealand Order of Merit for services to literature.

Fiona Farrell lives at Otanerito on Banks Peninsula. Her publications include two collections of short stories, two collections of poetry and four novels. *The Skinny Louie Book* received the New Zealand Book Award for Fiction in

1992, *The Hopeful Traveller* was runner up for the Deutz Medal in 2002 and *Book Book* was shortlisted for the 2005 Montana Book Awards. Her poetry has appeared in many anthologies (most recently in Roger McGough's *Wicked Poems*), has been set to music, and has featured as a set text for scholarship and GCSE exams. Fiona Farrell was awarded the Mansfield Fellow in Menton in 1995 and the Rathcoola Residency in southern Eire in 2006.

Beryl Fletcher has published short stories and a volume of memoir, *The House at Karamu*. Her first novel won a regional Commonwealth Writers Prize for Best First Book. She has been the recipient of Creative New Zealand project grants and has held three Writers in Residence in the United States of America and New Zealand. Her books have been translated into German and Korean.

Janet Frame, New Zealand's most distinguished writer, was born in Dunedin in 1924. She was the author of eleven novels, a three-volume autobiography, five collections of stories, a volume of poetry and a children's book. Also a lifelong cat-lover, Janet Frame's cats — and those of her family and friends — were a significant part of her life. Janet recorded 'The Cat of Habit' in 2002 for the Aotearoa/New Zealand Poetry Sound Archive, and she chose this to be played at her funeral in January 2004. 'The Cat of Habit' will also appear in a new collection of her poems, *The Goose Bath*, to be published by Random House/Vintage in 2006.

Paula Green is the current University of Auckland literary fellow. She is the author of three collections of poetry including, most recently, *Crosswind* (AUP, 2004). Her forthcoming anthology of poetry for children, *Flamingo Bendalingo*, is due 2006 and includes illustrations by artist Michael Hight.

Kevin Ireland lives in Devonport, on Auckland's North Shore. His fifteenth book of poems, *Walking the Land*, was published in 2003. This was preceded by his two memoirs, *Under the Bridge & Over the Moon*, and *Backwards to Forwards*. His fourth novel, *Getting Away with It*, was published in 2004, followed in 2005 by an extended essay, *On Getting Old*, and *How to Catch a Fish*. He was made an honorary DLitt by Massey University in 2000, and in 2004 he became the second recipient of the Prime Minister's Award for Poetry.

Stephanie Johnson is the author of six novels, five stage plays, two volumes of poetry and three collections of short stories, most recently *Drowned Sprat and other Stories* (2005). Her several awards and fellowships include the Deutz Medal for Fiction (for *The Shag Incident*, 2003) and she is the co-founder and co-creative director of the Auckland Readers and Writers Festival. While Stephanie is still mourning the loss of Scoundrel — best-loved cat, whose ashes reside on her mantelpiece — she shares her home with Scamp (who was raised with an eyedropper) and Venus.

Jan Kemp's sixth collection of poems *Dante's Heaven* is forthcoming from Puriri Press, Auckland, 2005. She is founding director of the Aotearoa New Zealand Poetry Sound Archive 2004. Her favourite cats are those which like poems, can let themselves out & go on the town. Not to forget Salty, black & white and most independent, basking under the snowball tree on a Morrinsville lawn, next to an outstretched dachshund, Peppy; both named & lovingly photographed by her elder brother Peter on his now-extinct Box Brownie.

Fiona Kidman has written more than twenty books, mainly novels and short stories. Her most recent release is a historical novel, *The Captive Wife* (Vintage, 2005). She also edits the annual anthology, *The Best New Zealand Fiction*, published by Vintage. She has been awarded a number of prizes and fellowships, and in 1998 was made a Dame Commander of the New Zealand Order of Merit for her services to literature. Fiona Kidman lives in Wellington.

Shonagh Koea lives in Auckland and likes going to the cinema. She is the author of eight novels, most lately *Time for a Killing* (Vintage, 2001) and *Yet Another Ghastly Christmas* (Vintage, 2003), and three short story collections. She was awarded the Fellowship in Literature at the University of Auckland in 1993 and the Buddle Findlay Sargeson Fellowship in 1997.

Gary Langford was born in Christchurch and is the author of twenty-four books (twenty-one published in Australia, three published in New Zealand), including nine novels and three collections of stories, the most recent being *Lunch at the Storyteller's Restaurant*, Hazard Press, 2002. He has also written many productions for the stage, radio and television in both countries. Gary is currently based in both Melbourne and Christchurch.

Graeme Lay has published several novels, short story collections and young adult novels, two of which were finalists in the New Zealand Post Children's Book Awards. Graeme also devised and edited the best-selling *100 New Zealand Short Short Stories* and co-edited a new collection, *Home* (Random House, 2005). *The Miss Tutti Frutti Contest — Travel Tales of the South Pacific*, was published in 2004 and his historical novel, *Alice & Luigi*, will appear in 2006. Graeme was the inaugural Writer in Libraries in Manukau city and is also Secretary of the Frank Sargeson Trust. Married with three adult children, Graeme's interests are reading, travel, photography and the sea.

Margaret Mahy was born in Whakatane in 1936. She wrote her first story when she was seven years old, printing it out very carefully and sewing the pages together. She wrote industriously for many years for children's columns in newspapers, and in 1961 her stories were published in the *New Zealand School Journal*. In 1969 she had five picture books published simultaneously. She is now the author of over a hundred and eighty books for children. Her various awards include the Carnegie Medal (twice), and the Esther Glen Medal (six times). Margaret is probably the oldest active writer for children in New Zealand, but hopes to write even more books over the next few years.

Katherine Mansfield (1888–1923) was born in Wellington, New Zealand and studied at Queen's College in London. After a brief return to New Zealand, Mansfield was back in London, determined to become a writer. She published *In a German Pension* in 1911, followed by *Bliss* (1920) and *The Garden Party* (1922). By this time her reputation as a fine short story writer was assured but she had been battling pulmonary tuberculosis, which she sought to escape by long stays in France. *The Doves' Nest* and *Something Childish and Other Stories*, were collected, edited and published after her death in 1923.

Owen Marshall has written and edited twenty books, most recently *Watch of Gryphons* (2005). Awards for his fiction include fellowships at the universities of Canterbury and Otago, and the Katherine Mansfield Memorial Fellowship in Menton, France. In 2000 he received the ONZM for services to literature, and his novel *Harlequin Rex* won the Montana New Zealand Book Awards Deutz Medal for Fiction. In 2002 the University of Canterbury awarded him the honorary degree of Doctor of Letters, and he was the inaugural recipient of the Creative New Zealand Writers' Fellowship in 2003.

Jeffrey Masson, former Sanskrit scholar and Projects Director of the Sigmund Freud Archives, has written over twenty books, including the bestsellers *When Elephants Weep* (1996), *Dogs Never Lie about Love* (1998), *The Nine Emotional Lives of Cats* (2002) and *The Pig Who Sang to the Moon* (2003). He lives by the sea in Auckland with his wife, two sons and three cats. Masson's cats accompany him every night on his walk along the shore, and he believes that with no other animal it is easier and more enchanting to cross the species barrier.

Emma Neale is the author of three novels, *Night Swimming, Little Moon* and *Double Take*, and two collections of poetry, *Sleeve-notes* and *How to Make a Million*, all published by Random House. Her current household familiar is a long-haired, black cannonball called Dangermouse.

Besides being one of New Zealand's foremost historians, **W. H. Oliver** has published several books of poetry, history and biography, including a memoir *Looking for the Phoenix* (2002) and *Poems 1946–2005* (2005). He has also edited *The Oxford History of New Zealand* (1981) and the first volume of *The Dictionary of New Zealand Biography* (1990).

Vincent O'Sullivan is a fiction writer, poet, biographer and playwright. He is the author of two novels — *Let the River Stand* (winner of the Montana Book Awards, 1994), and *Believers to the Bright Coast* (runner up for the Deutz Medal for Fiction, 1999) — a biography of John Mulgan, and many plays, collections of short stories and poems. He won the Montana Poetry Prize for *Seeing You Asked* in 1999 and *Nice Morning for it, Adam* in 2005. Vincent O'Sullivan was the Katherine Mansfield fellow in 1994, awarded the Creative New Zealand Michael King Writers' Fellowship in 2004 and was made a Distinguished Companion of the ONZM in 2000.

Vivienne Plumb is based in Wellington and writes poetry, prose and drama. She has been the recipient of several awards including the Hubert Church Prose Award, the Bruce Mason Playwrighting Award, and a Buddle Findlay Sargeson Fellowship. During 2004 she held an international writing residency at the University of Iowa, USA. Her most recent publication is a collection of poetry entitled *Nefarious* (Headworx Press, 2004), in which 'The Cinematic Experience' appears, and *Scarab*, a chapbook of a dozen poems, will be published in August, 2005 (Seraph Press).

Sarah Quigley is a novelist, poet and critic. She has a doctorate from the University of Oxford, and has won many awards for her poetry and short fiction, including the Commonwealth Pacific Region Short Story Award. In 2000 she won the inaugural Creative New Zealand Berlin Writer's Residency. Recent books include a collection of poetry, *Love in a Bookstore or Your Money Back* (AUP), and novels *Shot* and *Fifty Days*, both published by Virago. For the past five years she has been based in Berlin, where she is working on a new novel.

Frank Sargeson, 1903–1982, was the first major New Zealand writer to remain in this country. In electrifying fashion, he turned the language and rhythms of everyday speech into a new literary form. His themes show the compassion and understanding of working people and can also reveal a darkness lurking beneath ordinary exteriors. In accord with Sargeson's lifelong generosity to other writers, the Sargeson Trust has preserved his cottage in Takapuna, and awards Buddle Findlay Sargeson Fellowships to writers annually.

Elizabeth Smither's most recent collections of poems are *Red Shoes* (Te Mata Poet Laureate 3, Godwit, 2003) and *A Question of Gravity; Selected Poems* (Arc Publications, 2004). Straus, her ginger tomcat, follows a tradition of naming cats after publishers.

C. K. Stead was Professor of English at the University of Auckland until 1986. In 1984, he was awarded a CBE for services to New Zealand literature. He is the renowned author of poetry, of literary criticism and of short stories. He edited the Penguin Modern Classics *Letters and Journals of Katherine Mansfield* (1977). *Mansfield*, his tenth novel, was a runner up for the Deutz Medal for Fiction in the Montana New Zealand Book Awards 2005.

Philip Temple is the author of many works of fiction and non-fiction, as well as children's books, television documentaries — and the occasional poem. His latest publication is *White Shadows, Memories of Marienbad.* His books have won a number of prizes and he has been granted a variety of fellowships, most recently the Creative New Zealand Berlin Writers Residency 2003–2004. In 2004 Philip was awarded the ONZM for his services to literature.

Brian Turner's many books include poetry, sporting biographies and a memoir, *Somebodies and Nobodies* (Random House, 2002). He was the

Te Mata Estate New Zealand Poet Laureate 2003–2005. Brian's most recent books are *Footfall* (Random/Godwit, 2005), a collection of poems written during his term as poet laureate, and *Inside*, an account of the contentious career of All Black captain Anton Oliver, written in collaboration with Oliver (Hachette Livre, 2005).

Hone Tuwhare (1922–) is of Ngāpuhu, Ngāti Korokoro, Tautahi, Uri o Hau, Te Popoto and Scottish descent. He is perhaps New Zealand's most colourful and much-loved writer. His first collection of poetry, *No Ordinary Sun*, was first published in 1964 and has since been reprinted 12 times. He has twice won the Montana New Zealand Poetry award (1998, 2002) and has been awarded two honorary doctorates (University of Otago 1998 and University of Auckland 2005). Tuwhare is listed as one of ten Icon Artists by the Arts Foundation of New Zealand and in 2003 received the Prime Minister's Award for Literary Achievement for his outstanding contribution to New Zealand literature.

Peter Wells lives in Auckland with his cat, Miss Flounce. She came into his life after being abandoned over the Christmas holidays. She is a long-haired cat of considerable temperament. When he is not looking after his cat, Peter Wells writes books and makes films. His memoir, *Long Loop Home*, won the 2002 Montana New Zealand Book Award for Biography and his novel, *Iridescence*, was runner up for the Deutz Medal at the 2004 Montana New Zealand Book Awards.

Douglas Wright was born in Tuakau in 1956 and has worked in dance for over twenty-five years. He has created numerous works of dance-theatre which have been performed throughout New Zealand, Australia, in Europe and New York. In 2000 he was one of five inaugural laureates chosen by the Arts Foundation of New Zealand. His memoir *Ghost Dance*, published in 2004, won the E. H. McCormick Prize at the Montana Book Awards 2005. His new work of dance-theatre *Black Milk* will premiere in March 2006.

acknowledgements

The publishers gratefully acknowledge the authors, publishers, libraries, literary agencies and copyright holders for permission to reproduce the following works. AUP = Auckland University Press, VUP = Victoria University Press, OUP = Oxford University Press.

'A Blessing in Disguise' © Paula Green 2005

'A Cat Called Straus' and 'Listening to Handel with a Cat' © Elizabeth Smither, taken from *Red Shoes*, Godwit, 2003

'A Golden Cat' © Janet Frame Literary Trust, first published in 1967 by George Braziller, from *Janet Frame Stories and Poems: The Lagoon & Other Stories*; *The Pocket Mirror*, Vintage 2004

'A Personal Narrative' © Fiona Kidman 2005

'Alcatraz: Marital Property' © Barbara Else 2005

'Brute Instinct' © Emma Neale, taken from *Sleeve-notes*, Godwit, 1999

'Cat as Memoir' © Beryl Fletcher 2005

'Cat House' © Stephanie Johnson 2005

'Cat/ullus' © C. K. Stead, taken from *Dog Poems*, AUP, 2002

'Cat' © W. H. Oliver, taken from *Poems 1946–2005*, VUP, 2005

'Cats I have Known' © Peter Bland 2005

'Catsitting' © Diane Brown and Philip Temple 2005

'Fever' and 'Familiar' © Emma Neale, taken from *How to Make a Million*, Godwit, 2002

'Garden-lion', 'Crisis' and 'Admonition' by Ursula Bethell were first published in *From a Garden in the Antipodes*, London by Sidgwick & Jackson, 1929, under the pseudonym Evelyn Hayes

'King Canary, Queen Cat' © Kevin Ireland, taken from *Skinning a Fish*, Hazard Press, 1994

'Kitten' © Hone Tuwhare, taken from *Short Back and Sideways*, Godwit, 1992

'Landing on Their Feet' © Graeme Lay 2005

'lives and lives — the overlap cats' © Janet Charman 2005

'Mastersinger' © Bernard Brown, first published in *Victims and Traders*, Mallinson Rendel, 1980

'Monkey' © Martin Edmond 2005

'Morning Delivery' © Brian Turner 2005

'My Dear Gabrielle' © Peter Wells 2005

'Night Poem' © Jan Kemp

'On Attending the Death of a Cat' © Peter Wells 2005

'Q: So Where Do all the Cicadas Go?' © Sarah Quigley 2005

'Sale Day' © Frank Sargeson Literary Trust, taken from *The Stories of Frank Sargeson*, Penguin, 1986

'Sleeping Cat' and 'Straus after General Anaesthesia, Dental Extraction and Paw Examination' © Elizabeth Smither 2005

'Small' © Shonagh Koea 2005

'Sufficient Pussy' © Bernard Brown, taken from *Surprising the Slug*, Cape Catley, 1996

'The Cat Climbs' © Fiona Farrell, taken from *Cutting Out*, AUP, 1988

'The Cat of Habit' © Janet Frame Literary Trust 2005

'The Cat on the Mat and the Man Watching' © Vincent O'Sullivan, taken from *Nice Morning for it, Adam*, VUP, 2004

'The Cat Who Became a Poet' © Margaret Mahy 1982, published with kind permission of Margaret Mahy and Watson Little Ltd, London

'The Cinematic Experience' © Vivienne Plumb, taken from *Nefarious*, HeadworX, 2004

'The Couple Who Barbecue Cats' © Gary Langford, taken from *Lunch at the Storyteller's Restaurant*, Hazard Press, 2002

'The Human Miaow' © Douglas Wright 2005

'Thinking of Bagheera' © Owen Marshall, taken from *The Master of Big Jingles and Other Stories*, John McIndoe, 1982

'Tomcat' © J. C. Baxter, taken from *Collected Poems*, OUP, 1979

'Waiting for Rongo' © Vincent O'Sullivan 2005

Extract from 'Cats and Dogs' © Brian Turner 2002

Extract from 'Love' © Jeffrey Masson, taken from *The Nine Emotional Lives of Cats: A Journey into to the Feline Heart*, Vintage, 2004

Extracts from Katherine Mansfield's letters taken from *Katherine Mansfield: Letters and Journals*, selected by C. K. Stead, Vintage 2004

Jacket illustration: Frances Mary Hodgkins 1869–1947, 'Frances Hodgkins' letter to Isabel Hodgkins featuring the Black Devil, her cat' [ca 7 May 1892], ink sketch, from Manuscripts & Archives Collection, MS-Papers-0085-01-05, Alexander Turnbull Library, Wellington, New Zealand

Internal illustration: Frances Mary Hodgkins 1869–1947, 'Cat. 1920–1940', Ink on paper 45 x 83 mm, from Drawing & Prints Collection — Hodgkins, A-032-036, Alexander Turnbull Library, Wellington, New Zealand

Index of Titles and Authors